I0540940

Stuckey's Gold
The Curse of
Lake Juzan

Lori Crane

Lori Crane

Lori Crane Entertainment
www.LoriCrane.com

This book is a work of historical fiction. Some names, characters, places, and incidents are from historical accounts. Some names, characters, places, and incidents are products of the author's imagination.

ISBN 978-0990312031
eBook ISBN 978-0990312048

Table of Contents

Stuckey's Gold

The Curse of

Lake Juzan

Part I: The Story Begins

Seabirds cackled overhead and a whippoorwill sang in the top of a massive moss-covered oak that stood in the field behind the dilapidated wooden shack. The oak had been there more the one hundred years. The shack looked as if had been there the same amount of time. Its outer walls had bleached and cracked over the decades as it sat unsheltered in the unforgiving Mississippi sun. It held no paint on its walls. He liked it that way. Bland and inconspicuous. The front porch was covered by a drooping roof held up at its corners by bare two-by-sixes. The roof sagged dangerously in the middle, but it wouldn't fall as long as no one bumped the posts.

On the porch were three paint-pealed rocking chairs that had seen better days. He sat in one of them, slowly rocking back and forth, the chair creaking a monotonous song against the bare plank porch. The wrinkles surrounding his eyes showed the wisdom of his nearly sixty years, and they deepened as he squinted across the post-harvest field at the mighty Mississippi. She flowed swiftly by, ignoring him.

Two blond boys noisily appeared from around the corner,

cackling like chickens, racing to reach the porch. They jumped up onto the side of the porch, not bothering to use the two stone steps in front.

"Daddy said you wanted to see us," the older boy panted.

He stopped rocking and narrowed his eyes at the youngsters. "Yes, I did." He paused for a moment and the boys waited. "I wanted to talk to you about the curse of Lake Juzan. Ever heard of it?"

The boys both nodded.

"Well, your daddy and I have decided it's time for you two to hear the real story. How old are you now?"

"I'm twelve."

"And I'm ten."

"Well, have a seat right there, and I'll tell you the story."

He watched the boys climb into the same rocker, even though they could have used the two empty chairs. They wiggled and squirmed against each other until they got comfortable. Sitting side by side with their bare feet, dirty faces, and skinned knees, they looked so much like their father. As he looked at them, a light breeze rustled their hair and their blue eyes grew wide in anticipation.

He tore his attention away from the youngsters and gazed across the river, studying the storm clouds forming many miles away. He decided to start at the very beginning. He took and deep breath and sighed.

"Once upon a time, there was a fearless and mighty warrior. He was very young for an army captain at only twenty-five years old, but he led his troops with great skill and bravery. He commanded two hundred men at the Battle of New Orleans." He looked at the boys. "That was the last big battle of the War of 1812. You see, the British had been trying to occupy New Orleans for months and the Americans were determined to stop

them.

"The young captain led his troops into battle at the Chalmette Plantation in December of 1814. That was almost one hundred fifty years ago." He looked back at the river, deep in thought, as he continued. "The plantation was surrounded by marsh land, so his men couldn't take cover. They decided to simply crawl across the swampy land on their bellies. They lay still like logs so the British couldn't see them, and then ever so slowly, they inched closer and closer to the unsuspecting British camp. When they finally attacked at such close range, they easily defeated their enemy, shooting down every single British soldier who had dared encroach upon American soil.

"No one was more proud of the clever soldiers than their young captain. His name was Pierre Juzan."

Lori Crane

Chapter 1

Pierre Juzan's men showed their shrewdness and skill on the battlefield again and again. After their victory at Chalmette Plantation, their bravery was displayed a month later, in January of 1815, when British forces attacked Fort St. Philip. Pierre's men were trapped in the fort and bombarded by British cannon fire for ten days. They fought back with great tenacity, but after days of no sleep and running short on supplies, his men were tiring. Pierre had never lost a battle before and refused to do so now, so he eagerly joined the front lines to fight alongside his hungry and exhausted men.

He crawled through the muddy trench that ran outside the fort's stone walls, and he planted himself behind a dirt fortification where his men were being hit the hardest. He peeked over the earthen mound and saw at least a dozen Red Coats firing upon his soldiers. He turned and sat down in the trench to load his rifle. With the ground soaked from the last two days of rain, his clothing quickly became caked with red mud. The only things more abundant than the mud were the flies. He ignored the annoying insects buzzing around his head as he loaded his weapon, taking great pains to keep the muck from his rifle and ammunition. Over and over, the enemy fired its cannons, and dirt and mud flew around his men like a summer rain shower. He wiped it from his eyes with the back of his hand.

After he loaded, he looked over the hill, aimed at the enemy, and fired. A Red Coat instantly dropped to the ground like a rag doll. Success! He turned and sat down to reload.

A soldier next to him congratulated him, "Nice shot, Cap'n."

Pierre didn't acknowledge the comment. His hands moved quickly, focused on the task before him, knowing there were more Red Coats to dispose of.

He quickly rose and aimed again at the group of enemy soldiers and fired, but this time he didn't see whether or not his shot took down another Red Coat, because a blinding pain pierced his right temple. A fire-hot bullet had grazed him, spinning him to the right and momentarily blinding him. He fell backward and landed on his side. He heard a distinct snapping sound upon impact and felt excruciating pain in his shoulder. He tried to focus his eyes but it was extremely difficult to remain conscious. The pain on his temple and in his shoulder made him see stars. He reached up and touched his temple and felt the warm stickiness of warm blood oozing from the wound.

"Captain's been hit!" he heard one of his men yell.

"No, I'm all right. Continue fighting," he called back, but an ear-splitting cannon shot drowned out his command.

Dirt whirled like a tornado as the cannonball made impact right behind him. He pushed himself up to his hands and knees and tried to rise to his feet, but he was dizzy from pain and further blinded by flying debris.

"Keep fighting!" he yelled as he crawled in the direction of the trench.

He climbed down into the trench and inched toward the fort, still on his hands and knees, wincing with each agonizing movement. Each rifle and cannon fire sent waves of agony through his throbbing head and nausea through his stomach. His right shoulder felt like it was on fire. He knew he had dislocated or broken it in the fall. Bullets landed in the dirt all around him and he wondered how it was possible he had not been hit again. He wished for the right side of his body to go numb as he crept forward, inch by inch.

He was no more than twenty feet from the wall of the fort when he felt a heavy boot kick him in the ribs. It flipped him onto his back and knocked the air out of his lungs. He looked up into the crazed face of a British soldier. The man had a bayonet pointed at Pierre's chest. Pierre lay still and looked into the bloodshot eyes of his enemy, a thin and frightened man who was about to end his short life. There was nothing he could do except die as a brave man. There was no way to fight off this Red Coat. He forgot about the pounding in his skull and the pain in his shoulder as he gasped for his next breath, causing a sharp pain in his ribs where the boot had made the impact.

He refused to close his green eyes as he watched his enemy coil his arms backwards in preparation to stab Pierre's heart. Unexpectedly, someone appeared from behind the man and swiftly and deliberately brought down a machete on the man's head. Pierre braced for the weight as the British soldier fell directly onto him, the bayonet missing him by mere inches. Pierre looked up at his savior and saw it was one of his own soldiers, a black-haired man covered in splotches of red mud from head to toe.

"Are you all right, sir?" the soldier asked breathlessly.

"I think my ribs are broken now," Pierre grabbed his side and moaned, blood pouring down the side of his face, pooling on the ground beneath his head.

"That's not all that's wrong, sir. Let me get you to the surgeon."

The man lifted Pierre without struggle and carried him like a baby through the cannon fire all the way to the field hospital. It had to be at least a mile from the fort, but the fearless soldier marched on undeterred.

He carried Pierre into the humid and reeking surgeon's tent and gently placed him on a wooden chair. Pierre winced as his arm fell limply at his side.

"You're in good hands now, sir. I have to return to my comrades. This battle will be ours."

Pierre couldn't reply. He was thankful for the soldier's strength and tenacity, but he was beginning to feel the first effects of the horrific incident that almost ended his life. He trembled uncontrollably as shock set in. The medical team surrounded him to tend to his wounds so he didn't witness the soldier exit the tent, but he vowed to find out who the young man was and to thank him as soon as he was able.

He was moved to a cot for examination. There he lay silent, trying to breathe and not tremble, as a nurse covered him in a blanket and cleaned and stitched his head wound. He stared at the roof of the tent, genuinely surprised by the turn of events. It had never before occurred to him that he could die on the battlefield, but he'd been sure he was about to do just that in this battle. That brave soldier had saved him.

Pierre owed the man his life.

Chapter 2

A few days later, after the battle had ended and the British had fled New Orleans, Leon Fisher was summoned to Pierre's tent. When he arrived, he found Pierre sitting up in a straight-backed wooden chair. A lantern glowed on a table in the middle of the tent, flooding it with soft golden light. Except for the bandage on the side of Pierre's head and his arm in a sling, Pierre looked surprisingly well. He smiled when the soldier entered the tent.

"Come in, Private, and have a seat." With his good arm, Pierre gestured toward the wooden chair adjacent to him. "You look a lot better when you're not covered in mud." Pierre chuckled.

"Thank you, sir," Leon mumbled and awkwardly sat down. He wanted to say the captain look better also, but he was unsure if that would be appropriate. He wasn't accustomed to being called before an officer, and he had certainly never been summoned to a casual or social meeting with one.

Pierre gestured to the young lad in the doorway,

who poured and served some whiskey, handing the first glass to Pierre and the second to Leon. Pierre raised his glass in a toast. Leon followed suit.

"I'd like to formally thank you for saving my life, and I'd like to make a toast to a new and lifelong friendship."

Leon nodded politely and they downed the brown liquid.

Pierre sighed as the whiskey burned the back of his throat, and then he leaned forward and placed his glass on the small round table between them. He reclined back in his chair and grimaced as he stretched out his legs and crossed his ankles. "So, tell me about yourself," he urged.

Leon had never before had anyone interested in his life. There wasn't much to tell, nothing that he wanted to share anyway. He looked down at the floor to hide his embarrassment. "Well, my name is Leon Fisher."

"Very well, Leon. What else?"

"Um...I was born in Chunky, Mississippi. My people call it Chanki Chitto."

"You're Choctaw? I should have guessed." Pierre slapped his thigh and let out a small chuckle.

Leon slumped in his chair ever so slightly. In his experience, his people were generally not treated well by the white man. Though he had the dark features of an Indian, he always played them down and told everyone his family was from Italy. He never, ever told anyone he was Choctaw, and he didn't know what had possessed him to be honest with this man.

The captain smiled. "My mother was Choctaw. My father was French. That's where my name comes from. It's Pierre."

Leon breathed a sigh of relief. Perhaps the captain would not demote him to cleaning officers' boots.

Pierre continued, "All of my mother's family is from that same area around Chanki Chitto. You and I should plan to get together after this war is over. We can have our families meet."

"I'm afraid I don't have any family left, sir. The Great Spirit has not seen fit to bless us with longevity. But I'd be happy to meet your wife and family."

"Oh, I'm not married, but I do have my eye on a young lady back home. I think after the war is over, I'd like to open a small inn and tavern near the lake on my family's property. I'm going to marry that young lady and live a peaceful and prosperous life. How about you, Leon? What are your plans following the war?"

"I haven't rightly given it much thought, sir."

"Well, you should come and work for me. I owe you for saving my life. Oh, hell, you shouldn't work *for* me, you should work *with* me. We could become business partners. What do you think of that idea?"

Leon was stunned. Who would have ever imagined him as a partner in a business? He nodded eagerly. "I would be honored to work with you, sir."

"All right then, it's settled. But the first thing you must do is stop calling me sir. Call me Pierre. After all, we're business partners now."

"Yes, sir...I mean Pierre," Leon muttered as he shook Pierre's extended hand.

Pierre leaned back with a groan and stretched his legs out in front of him again, and the two shared another couple rounds of whiskey. They talked deep into the evening, discussing plans for their new business venture and becoming fast friends.

Within weeks, the war ended.

Chapter 3

Following the war, Leon and Pierre returned to their hometown of Chunky, Mississippi, and spent the next five years building an inn and tavern among the pines on the shores of Lake Juzan, named after Pierre's family. From the first day they opened their doors, they knew the inn would be a great success. With their unique personalities, they couldn't have been better partners. Pierre was outgoing and friendly, the consummate host with an ever-present smile on his face. Leon was quiet and soft spoken with an uncanny knack for knowing what the guests needed before they even asked. He made every guest feel comfortable and valued.

Once the inn became successful, Pierre married the young lady he had been courting. Her name was Catherine and she was a beautiful young woman, half Choctaw, half English. She spent most of her time cooking for the guests at the tavern and putting badly needed feminine touches in the rooms at the inn. She filled them with flowers, wall hangings, and hand-sewn down pillows, but she was so busy seeing to the daily needs of the guests, she didn't have time to do time-consuming tasks like weave rugs or sew quilts, so she paid an Indian girl over in Chunky to make these items. The young Indian maiden's name was Eula, and when she came to the inn for the first time to deliver the quilts and rugs, Catherine asked Leon to unload them from her wagon.

"Good afternoon, miss," Leon called to her as he approached the wagon. "Catherine asked me to unload some items from your wagon."

At the sound of his voice, Eula turned to face him and froze. She blushed when she saw the handsome Indian approaching her. The sun glistened on his black hair which was tied in a braid and hung around his shoulder down onto his muscular chest. He wore a simple vest with no shirt, and his well-defined arms were bare. His eyes twinkled with kindness and warmth, and his smile was gentle. She had never before seen such a striking man, and she couldn't help but smile back at him.

Leon almost tripped over his own feet when she turned. She was undoubtedly the most beautiful woman he had ever seen. Her turquoise blue mantle glowed against her chocolate skin and black hair, and when she smiled, his heart felt like it exploded.

It was love at first sight for both of them.

Eula was a dainty woman of Choctaw heritage who had a smile like the midday sun. She brightened up every room she entered, and Leon thought she was incredibly lovely. The second time Eula came to the inn to drop off rugs and quilts, she stayed for a few days, and as Leon got to know her, he fell head over heels. There couldn't have been a more perfect match than

Eula and Leon. They married within weeks of her second visit, and Leon built them a cottage behind the inn so they could have plenty of privacy away from the guests and Pierre and Catherine.

Within the next few years, both Catherine and Eula had both delivered healthy sons. Pierre and Leon couldn't have been more proud. They named the boys Gabriel Juzan and Martin Fisher—good strong names for good strong boys.

Nearly a decade earlier, Pierre had almost died on the battlefield, and Leon saved his life. Nearly a decade earlier, Leon had no family or future. Now he had a wife and a fine son. His prospects had been turned around by Pierre's kindness and friendship. The couples raised their sons, worked long hours at the inn, and life was very good. The four of them had become the closest of friends, all finding their niche in the family business.

Daily, Pierre poured over his business journals. He logged every customer, every beer served, every dollar made. No one was more meticulous about record keeping than Pierre. He was always searching for improvements and shortcuts, always looking for better and easier ways to make more money, and always coming up with imaginative ideas to increase his profits.

One of Pierre's notions was to offer Leon's services as a hunting and fishing guide. No one knew the woods and the lake better than Leon, and Leon certainly didn't mind getting away from the clamor of the inn to escort customers on expeditions. Not only did Leon's services make money, they also contributed to suppers at the tavern. The guests were always delighted when the meal had been provided by one of the other guests and expertly prepared by Pierre's loving wife, Catherine.

Another idea Pierre came up with was to peddle Eula's rugs and quilts. When guests remarked on the beautiful furnishings in their rooms, Pierre always offered them copies to take home—for a hefty price, of course. He especially liked to sell items to male travelers to take home as gifts for their wives and had even received a few thank you notes from those happy women.

The one thing Pierre refused to change was the alcohol he sold in the tavern. He would never water his booze down like the taverns in town did. He enjoyed it when late evening came and he could entice his drunken guests into a friendly game of poker. After he won all their money and the sun began to rise, they would often be too drunk or hungover to travel, so he would get an extra day's lodgings out of them on top of the winnings.

Chapter 4

Late one evening, all but one of the guests had retired for the night. Pierre was wiping down the bar top and Leon was sweeping up the tavern. The loner sat quietly at the end of the bar. He'd arrived alone that afternoon and had not spoken to anyone all evening. He was scheduled to depart the next day.

"Can I get you another drink, sir?" Pierre offered.

"Sure. Just one more. I have a busy day tomorrow." He rubbed his unshaven chin.

"Are you heading out early in the morning?"

"Uh, no, not until about noon. I'm guarding a coach that's traveling through the county. It's supposed to arrive at the county line about one o'clock, and I have to be there to meet it."

"Guarding a coach? That sounds like an interesting profession. What would be so important in a coach that it'd need to be guarded?"

The man downed the liquid Pierre placed in front of him. "Actually, there was supposed to be two of us but my partner didn't show up." The man leaned toward Pierre and whispered, "It's a bank coach filled with gold." The man slurred as he spoke. Obviously the alcohol was causing his tongue to wag, and he didn't even hesitate as he told the information to Pierre.

"Gold?" Pierre whispered back. "I thought banks sent gold by train."

"Oh, they used to, but with all the train robberies, some have started sending it by coach. The banks think it's a lot safer because nobody knows about it."

Pierre continued to wipe down the bar top. "Well, I guess they have a point. Nobody can steal it if they don't know about it, and I've never heard of that sort of thing."

The man nodded. "The banks are still very careful. They hire armed guards like me to escort the coaches through the counties. Usually one guard rides in front of the coach and one behind, and of course the two drivers are armed as well." The man hiccupped.

"But it's only you this time?"

"Yeah, I don't know what happened to my partner. I guess I'll have to stay in front and be extra careful." The man shrugged. "I'm not too worried about it though, because we never have any problems. Like I said, no one knows about it, well, no one except you now." The chuckled and pushed his glass toward Pierre for a refill.

Pierre laughed cordially as he poured the man another drink.

The man downed the whiskey and set the glass back down on the bar. Pierre began to refill it but the man waved his hand over his glass. "Oh, I should stop."

"No, this one's on the house. Enjoy."

"Well, if you insist." The man threw his head back and drank the liquid in one gulp.

Pierre pulled another glass off the shelf. "As a matter of fact, I think I'll join you in a nightcap." He filled both glasses to the rim. They toasted each other with a clink of their glasses, drank, and slammed their glasses down on the bar.

Leon approached them, broom in hand. "Hey, what are you fellas drinking to?"

Pierre pulled another glass off the shelf, placed it next to his and the patron's, and filled all three. "We're drinking to gold," he said and raised his glass again.

The patron chuckled and raised his glass. "To gold."

"To gold." Leon lifted his glass.

As Leon drank, he gazed over the rim of his glass at Pierre, as if questioning what the topic of the conversation was. Pierre shook his head ever so slightly, silently warning Leon to remain silent.

Many drinks and hours later, Pierre and Leon learned the impending coach contained a large trunk of gold bound for Mobile. It would be traveling from the northwest of the county to the southeast. The coach would look like a common traveler's wagon—with a canvas cover, two drivers, and pulled by two horses. It would pass right by Lake Juzan.

After the drunken man bid them a good evening and staggered out the door, Pierre and Leon sat at the bar and had one more drink.

Pierre placed his empty glass down on the bar and stared at it. "What would you think about meeting up with that wagon tomorrow?"

Leon looked at him with surprise. "What, and rob it?"

Pierre looked up, his eyes boring into Leon. "Sure." He shrugged and grinned. "Why not?"

Leon raised his eyebrows. Pierre took that as a yes. He pulled his business journal out from the shelf under the bar, opened it to an empty page, and sketched out a drawing of the road the coach would be traveling on. The two made a detailed plan to intercept the wagon and steal the gold.

By the time they retired for what was left of the night, they both knew tomorrow their lives would change forever.

Chapter 5

The next day, after their very hungover friend had departed from the inn, Pierre and Leon made excuses to their wives about some work that needed to be done on the other side of the lake, so they could disappear for a few hours with no one looking for them. They saddled up their fastest steeds and rode to the top of the hill, just around the other side of the lake. They would intercept the coach before it rounded the curve and headed down the hill toward Lake Juzan. They hid in the pine trees on either side of the road and waited. With the slant of the land, they could see all the way down to the glittering lake below.

The sun had already reached its highest point and was slowly beginning its descent behind them. By the look of the shadows, Leon guessed it was around three o'clock. He knew the traveling distance from the county line, so he figured the coach would be arriving at any moment. As he recalculated its arrival time, he heard horse hooves on the road. The two sat silent and still on their horses on either side of the road and watched the man from last night trot past them. Their plan was to let him travel by unharmed as to not warn the drivers of impending danger. They would take care of him later.

Not more than a few minutes had passed before they heard the grinding of the wagon's wheels. When it came into sight, Leon saw two men sitting in the front driver's seat of the wooden coach. One was whistling a tune. Leon was feeling anxious and wanted to get on with it, so he decided to make the annoying whistler his first target. He pulled out his bow, armed it with an arrow, took aim through the trees, and let his arrow fly. It hit its intended target and the whistling abruptly stopped. The whistler slumped in his seat, an arrow through the side of his neck. The horses didn't flinch, but the man's partner looked over at him and his jaw dropped. Leon quickly pulled out another arrow, aimed, and put it through the chest of the second man as he still stared at his partner in disbelief. The second man slumped in the seat.

From higher up on the hill, Pierre rode his horse out of the woods and fell in line behind the wagon. He gave Leon a nod. Leon nodded back. He tucked his bow away and emerged from the woods, trotting alongside the wagon. The wagon's team kept pulling the wagon forward, oblivious to the fact they no longer had a driver. They began to increase their speed as the road began to slant downhill. Leon grabbed the side of the wagon and pulled himself onto it, abandoning his own horse on the road. He crawled across the canvas back and climbed over the rail into the driver's seat. He grabbed the whistler by the front of his shirt and pushed him over the side. The man plopped onto the road like a sack of potatoes, and Leon felt the coach jostle and heard bones snap as the back wheel of the wagon ran over some part of the whistler's body. He grimaced at the sound.

Behind him, Pierre grabbed Leon's abandoned horse's reins and continued down the hill, pulling Leon's horse along with him. Leon glanced back and saw both horses whinny and rear up when they approached the whistler's body unexpectedly sprawled in the middle of the road.

He turned his attention back to the coach's horses. They were now nearing a gallop down the hill. He reached down on the floor of the wagon and fumbled around until he found the reins. He grabbed them and was about to sit up and pull back on them when the butt of a gun came down on top of his head. He saw stars as he fell to the floor of the coach. He turned his head and saw the whistler's partner pointing a revolver at his face. As the driver clicked the hammer back, Leon kicked the gun out of the man's hand. He heard it bounce off the edge of the wagon then discharge as it hit the ground. The sound echoed through the trees, startling the wagon's horses who took off at a full gallop.

Leon climbed to his feet and his assailant grabbed at him. He stepped over the front railing and out onto the tongue of the wagon, pulling the man with him. Leon held onto the tongue as the man lost his grip on Leon and fell between the horses. He landed on the ground and the wagon rolled over him. Pierre galloped up from behind and shot the man in the chest as he lay on the road.

Leon pulled himself back up and stood up on the tongue. He looked at Pierre and started to give him a thumbs up in thanks when suddenly a shot whizzed by his head. He saw Pierre's gun pointing straight at him, and for a moment, he thought Pierre was shooting at *him*. He followed Pierre's gaze and turned to see that Pierre had shot the man behind him. The man from last night had undoubtedly returned to see why shots had been fired. Leon watched him clutch his chest and fall from his horse. He fell off the drop-off and rolled down the hill, but his horse kept galloping straight toward the wagon.

On this particular stretch, the road narrowed between the bank of rocks on one side and the drop-off on the other. The man's horse and the wagon's team were heading directly toward each other, neither having a way to escape a collision.

They were about to crash when the wagon's team moved slightly to the right onto the very edge of the drop-off, and the guard's horse moved to the left, its saddle rubbing against the rock wall on one side and the wagon on the other. Leon breathed a sigh of relief as the man's horse passed the wagon. His relief was short lived, however, as he felt the wagon shift, its right wheels finding no road to rest its weight upon. It tilted dangerously to the right and Leon grabbed the horses' tails to keep from tumbling off the tongue. The horses panted and whinnied as they struggled to keep the wagon on the road. Leon climbed out onto the tongue as far as he could, frantically searching for the reins, which had been lost in the struggle with the driver.

He saw them! They were dangling between the horses, bouncing on the hard ground. Balancing himself on the tongue, holding a horse's tail with one hand, Leon groped with his other hand for the reins. He almost had them when the tongue came unhitched from the horses. The reins escaped his grasp as the horses, frightened by the shift in weight, galloped faster and veered left, back onto the road. He held onto the horse's tail for only a moment longer before it pulled away from his grasp. The road curved to the left, which is where the horses headed. The wagon continued moving in a straight line, soon leaving the edge of the road completely and roaring down the steep hill toward the lake. Leon held onto the tongue as tightly as he could, fearing if he fell, he would be crushed by the runaway wagon behind him. He heard Pierre yelling something, but he knew there was nothing he or Pierre could do to stop rolling wagon. He held on for his life as the wagon picked up speed, jostling him like a rag doll as it leaped over bushes and knocked down pine saplings. It felt as if the wheels would break off at any moment, but not before his insides shook themselves to death. When the coach reached the bluff, it left the hill, soaring through the air, ten feet above the surface of the lake.

Time seemed to move in slow motion as the wagon and Leon sailed through the air, but within moments, Leon and the wagon crashed with a mighty splash into the lake. The front wheels broke in half upon impact. The driver's seat broke in two across Leon's back. The wind was knocked out of him as he slammed into the water and again when he was crushed by the wagon. He was sure he had broken more than a few ribs and most of the fingers on his left hand, which was still holding on to the tongue of the wagon. It was no longer connected to the wagon, and it began dragging him under. He let go of it, kicked his legs, and his head broke the surface of the water. He felt a moment of relief as he gulped for air. He wanted to cry out in pain, but he couldn't get enough breath to do so. His chest screamed in agony as he filled his lungs with air. He was seriously hurt, but at least he was alive.

He turned in circles, looking at the destruction around him. Boards floated all around, but what was left of the wagon was still afloat. The canvas tarp darkened as it began to soak up water, and he knew the weight of the gold would quickly sink the wagon. With his right hand, he struggled to untie one side of the canvas top. After what seemed like forever, he pulled the canvas away from the wagon, which was now tilting as it filled with water. He got one quick glimpse of the coveted wooden trunk before it tipped on its side and fell off the wagon, allowing what was left of the wagon to bob as it straightened itself. Without thinking, Leon dove after the trunk and grabbed the handle, but it was too heavy. He couldn't stop the downward momentum and it pulled him into the depths. He reluctantly released the handle and swam back to the surface. He looked at the bluff to find Pierre.

Pierre sat on his horse on top of the bluff, watching the events unfold beneath him.

Leon took a deep breath through the stabbing pain in his chest and was about to yell to Pierre to come down and help when the wagon tilted and gurgled and began to sink. The rope from the canvas top wrapped around his leg and pulled him under. He frantically grabbed at the rope, but he couldn't free himself. The last thing he felt was water filling his lungs.

* * *

Pierre watched in horror as his precious cargo sank below the surface of the murky lake. He saw Leon dive for it but apparently he couldn't bring it up. Leon appeared above the surface of the water only for a moment, and he looked as if he was about to yell something when the wagon began to sink and Leon disappeared. It looked like something had pulled him under.

Pierre waited for Leon to reappear, but with each passing second, terror began to run like ice through his veins.

"Leon!" he yelled toward the water, but there was no answer. "Leon!!"

The ripples and waves caused by the wagon crashing into the lake had begun to subside. As the water grew still, Pierre realized too much time had passed. His friend was dying.

He turned his horse back to the road and galloped as fast as he could down the hill toward the dock. He jumped off his horse, climbed into one of the two small rowboats, and paddled across the lake as fast as he could to the place he had last seen Leon. As he approached the spot, he saw something floating in the water.

"Leon!" he screamed and rowed even faster.

Leon was floating face down in the black water. He didn't move.

Pierre cried as he pulled his friend's body into the boat and rowed back to the dock.

Chapter 6

The next day, as dark, gray thunderheads loomed above them, Eula and her fifteen-year-old son, Martin, watched the men lower Leon's body into a grave. Eula was inconsolable and Martin stared silently at the ground, his hand resting on his mother's shoulder. Pierre, Catherine, and their teenage son Gabriel, shed silent tears as they watched the proceedings. The minister said a final prayer and it was over. After hugging Eula and shaking hands with Martin, the minister left, leaving everyone to go about their day.

Pierre wanted to row out and retrieve the trunk but he knew the impending storms wouldn't allow it, so he reluctantly went to the tavern to ready it for the night's guests. Catherine went to the inn to clean. Eula asked Gabriel to take Martin out to the barn to tend the animals. She wanted to go back to her cottage and be alone for a while. She tried to keep herself occupied by working on her loom, but each time the thunder clapped, she jumped. The anxiety of losing her husband was multiplied by the unanswered questions surrounding his death.

Yesterday, she couldn't get any straight answers from Pierre, and something about his story didn't make sense. There was no way Leon drowned in the lake as Pierre claimed. Leon was a great swimmer and comfortable in the water. What were the two doing way out on the other side of the lake? And why was Leon's horse saddle up on the bluff and he down in the lake? Why wasn't his horse at the dock with Pierre's horse? She decided to find Pierre and ask him again.

She marched toward the tavern in the rain that was now coming down in sheets. She yanked the door open and yelled for Pierre.

"Pierre Juzan! Explain to me what happened to my husband," she demanded, rain dripping from her black hair down her face.

Pierre kept wiping down the tables and didn't look at her. "I already told you, Eula. He drowned in the lake."

She stomped toward him, hands on her hips. "That's impossible and you know it. He was a great swimmer. What was he doing in the lake when his horse was saddled up on the bluff?"

"Well, that's a little harder to explain." He moved quickly past her and walked around behind the bar.

"I suggest you try," she snapped.

He turned toward her and raised his voice. "And I'd suggest you curb your tone, woman." His green eyes were electric with anger.

She wanted to jump over the bar and slap him across the face, but she knew that behavior wouldn't get her the answers she so desperately needed. She lowered her head. "I'm sorry, Pierre. Why was my husband's horse on the bluff?"

He gestured toward the nearest table. "You should take a seat. It's a long story." He placed his cleaning rag on the bar and came out to sit with her at the table.

Pierre pulled up a chair and told Eula the whole story, from the talkative drunk at the tavern to Leon sinking with the wagon. Eula glared at him in disbelief but remained silent until he finished speaking.

"So, my husband died for a trunk of gold?"

"In the short version of the story, yes."

Eula rose to her feet and cried out, "Why didn't you save him?"

Pierre rose also. "I couldn't save him, Eula. I was on top of the bluff. And you're not the only one here who's upset. He was my best friend. He saved me a long time ago, and I couldn't return the kindness."

She started to breathe more heavily as her temper escalated. "You let my husband drown for a stupid trunk filled with some gold and you want me to feel sorry for you? How could you let this happen, Pierre? Leon was your friend for thirty years, and you sacrificed him for money? How dare you call him your friend? True friends would never do something like that."

Pierre reached out to place his hand on her shoulder but she jerked away from him as she continued. She rose to her feet and pointed her finger in his face. "I think I shall go to the sheriff and tell him what you've done. You deserve to hang for this, Pierre Juzan! You deserve to be as dead as my poor Leon."

Before Pierre could stop himself, he jumped up

from his chair, and his hand flew up and he backhanded Eula across the face, snapping her head to the side. She slowly turned back toward him, her wet hair hanging across her face, and she narrowed her eyes at him.

Pierre pointed his finger at her. "Eula, Leon *was* my friend. You need to mind your business, and if you *ever* raise your voice to me again, I will throw you off my land. Do I make myself clear?"

"My husband's death certainly *is* my business, and if you ever touch me again, you will pay for it," she growled.

"Is that a threat?"

"That, sir, is a fact." She spun toward the door.

Pierre also turned toward the door, except when he turned, he knocked over a chair. Eula took a step forward at that exact moment, tripped on the overturned chair, and fell to the floor. Pierre glanced back, but he didn't stop to help her up. He continued forward, pushed open the tavern door, and stomped out into the storm, leaving her lying on the floor and letting the door slam behind him.

Chapter 7

Eula was convinced Pierre knocked her down on purpose yesterday, just to show her he was the boss. She sat in the rocking chair on the front porch of her cottage and she rubbed her aching arm, which was now held firmly in a sling. The rain had not let up, and the threatening storm clouds matched her mood. She rocked furiously back and forth, deciding what she should do. The more she thought about her husband dying for gold, her arm being broken, and the threats Pierre made to kick her off his land, the more she swore she would make him pay.

Eula had grown up in the Choctaw village of Chanki Chitto, and as a young girl, her mother had taught her many things. She could weave and sew, farm and cook, but the most important things she knew, she learned from her grandmother. She learned the ways of the medicine woman, which not only included healing the sick and nurturing the young and elderly, but also taking down the enemy. She struggled to remember what her grandmother had taught her as she now had an enemy to deal with. How dare Pierre threaten her! He knew she had no place to go.

Ten years ago, Pierre Juzan was one of the men who in exchange for a large plot of land from the government signed the Treaty of Dancing Rabbit Creek. The treaty took all the land from the Choctaw, including Chanki Chitto, and bestowed it to the US government. In return, the government gave the Indians a new land called the Oklahoma Territory. In the months that followed, her entire village moved far away from Mississippi. It broke her heart to bid farewell to her mother and father and her beloved grandmother, but Eula couldn't join them on their journey because she had married Leon. Leon would never leave Pierre's side. They were running a successful business, and they just couldn't move away with the rest of the family, especially with a young son in tow. She sadly said goodbye to her family, knowing she would likely never see them again. She had to make a choice at the time, and she chose to stay with Leon and Martin. In doing so, she had remained on Pierre Juzan's land with no other place to go.

The more she replayed yesterday's confrontation in her head, the angrier she became with Pierre. Yes, she would make him pay. He would pay for everything. He would pay for his threats, for signing the treaty that took her family away, and most importantly—for Leon's death. She would make sure of it. Pierre's time of suffering was drawing nigh.

As darkness fell and the raging two-day storm had subsided, Eula ventured out to the lake under the light of the full moon. She pulled a candle from her cloak and lit it. She knelt on the sandy shore and placed the candle on a piece of bark. She carefully floated the bark on the water and gently pushed it out onto the still lake. Frogs croaked, and an owl called to her from the other side of the lake. Coyotes howled from the bluff.

She raised her good arm to the moon.

"Oh, Great Spirit, heed my desire. Bring forth your snakes, your water fowl, your poisonous spiders, your great wind, pale moon, burning sun, and your deepest, coldest water from the black, swampy lake to exact revenge on Pierre Juzan for taking one of your own. Curse his precious gold, so that whoever touches it will die as horribly as your great son, Leon Fisher. I curse the trunk of gold that lies on the bottom of this lake for all time henceforth and forever more."

The candle stopped in the middle of the lake and slowly began to spin. The winds picked up as new storm clouds blew in from the west. Thunder rumbled from the heavens. The moon disappeared behind thick ominous clouds, leaving the shore in pitch-blackness. The light of the candle could faintly be seen from the shore, and Eula was surprised it hadn't extinguished in the wind. She could see it spinning faster and faster as it bounced on the increasing waves. Suddenly, a lightning bolt zigzagged from the heavens to the candle, and for a split second, the entire lake lit up like midday. The candle exploded, sending sparks in every direction. Eula's jaw dropped at the spectacle. Then, just as quickly as the storm began, it instantaneously stopped. Everything became deathly still. The clouds dissipated as if they were never there. The wind became calm. The remains of the candle and the piece of bark sank out of sight.

The lake was eerily quiet. Even the coyotes, owls, and frogs had silenced. Eula stared at the black place where the candle had been. She watched as the ripples on the water instantly calmed to glass.

After a few minutes, she slowly rose to her feet, wiped the sand from her cloak, and ambled by the light of the moon back to her cottage behind the inn.

Chapter 8

As the sun began its rise into the clear blue sky the next morning, Pierre rowed his boat out to the place in the lake where he thought the trunk had sunk. Ducks splashed on the shoreline, and the balmy day was unclouded and beautiful. When he finally retrieved the treasure, it would officially be the best day of his life.

He tossed the anchor over the side and dove into the water again and again, bobbing up only for a breath of air, and then back down, feeling around for the trunk. He found bits and pieces of the wagon, but he was getting frustrated with the time it was taking to locate the treasure. After more than a dozen attempts, he finally felt the square shape of the trunk. Strangely, it was quite a ways from where he thought it would be. For a moment, he wondered if there was a current in the lake, but dismissed the thought. It was just a lake. Lakes didn't have currents.

He came up for air and dove down again to retrieve his gold. He fumbled with the lock on the front, but it was securely intact. He rose for another breath of air and swam down again. This time he grabbed the handle on one side and tried to lift it, but it was simply too heavy. He rose to the surface again and swam over to his boat. He climbed in and rowed it directly above the trunk. He dropped anchor again and grabbed the spare rope from the floor of the boat. He dove into the lake again, located the trunk, and tied the rope around the handle. He then swam back to the surface, climbed into the boat, and pulled on the rope, but the heavy trunk wouldn't give. With each pull, the boat listed dangerously to one side. He became more and more excited, thinking there must be an enormous amount of gold in the trunk to make it so heavy.

He decided the only way to bring it to the surface was to make a pulley system. He wrapped the rope around the middle of the bench that stretched across the boat's interior. He sat on the floor and planted his feet on either side of the bench with the rope between his legs. He wrapped the rope around his wrists and pulled with all his might. The rope gave a few inches as the gold lifted off the lake floor. It's going to work! He hoped the trunk hadn't been damaged in the crash and wouldn't be spilling out gold pieces as he pulled, but he knew even though it would be time consuming, it would be easier to retrieve the gold a piece at a time than to fight with the weight of the trunk. He wished there wasn't a lock on the damned thing. He believed it'd be better to try the pulley system before trying to pick the lock under water.

He braced himself and heaved again. Sweat dripped from his brow, stinging his eyes. He blinked and heaved again. The rope began to coil inch by inch in the bottom of the boat. He kept pulling. The rope came in about two feet. Another tug. Another foot. Another. He heard the trunk thump against the bottom of the boat. His heart pounded. He tied the rope around the bench and leaned over the edge of the boat. The boat tipped to the side and water splashed in over the edge. There it was! He could see the trunk just below the surface. He pulled on the rope that was now taut and the trunk thumped again against the bottom. That wasn't going to work. The angle was all wrong.

Pierre reached into the water and grabbed the handle with his right hand, nearly capsizing in the process. He pulled and pulled but it was no use. He had no leverage. On his knees, he leaned over the side of the boat and grabbed the handle with both hands. He leaned back as he adjusted himself and braced his feet against the inside of the boat. The small craft listed sharply. Next to him, he saw the taut rope go slack. It took him only a moment to realize the trunk had come untied. His adrenaline rose as he realized the only things now holding his precious gold were his tired arms and sheer determination. The boat was leaning almost on its side. Water sloshed in over the edge, filling the bottom. He held on even though his fingers were growing numb and his shoulders felt like they were pulling out of their sockets. He knew he didn't have much time. With a deep, guttural grunt, he gave one final tug. The very thing he'd been trying to avoid happened. His rowboat capsized. The trunk sank back to the bottom of the lake, and Pierre Juzan along with it. He tried to let go of the handle but couldn't open his cramped fingers. The force of the trunk hitting the bottom of the lake felt like a jolt of lightning reverberating up through his arms and into his shoulders. He again tried to let go of the handle, but there was a strange vibration in his fingers and they wouldn't open. He braced his feet against the trunk and pushed away from it, but it was no use. He looked up through the murky water at the surface. The sun glistened above, causing trails of light to dance through the water, surrounding him. With his last bit of air, he pulled one last time. It did no good.

The next day, his body was found floating on the surface of the black water.

Part II: The Curse Continues

"When the lake took the lives of Pierre Juzan and Leon Fisher within days of each other in 1841, their sons Gabriel and Martin were both a tender fifteen years old. They had been taught well by their fathers and easily stepped in to help their mothers run the inn. A few years later, Gabriel's mother, Catherine, came down with a terrible fever. Eula nursed her for a week, but Catherine passed peacefully in the dead of the night. After that, it was just Eula and the boys. But the curse wasn't finished yet, and even Eula couldn't foresee the horror that was to come."

The boys gawked at the old man, anticipating the next part of the story. He smoothly rocked back and forth, observing the great Mississippi before him. The humidity grew and the winds were starting to pick up as the clouds drew closer to the far side of the river. He knew they would get a good soaking before nightfall.

"What happened next?" asked the younger boy.

"Well, by the time Gabriel and Martin were both in their twenties, they were running the inn as a team and everything was going along just fine...for a while. Gabriel had married a French woman named Marguerite, and Martin had married an

English woman named Florence, whose family had disowned her for marrying an Indian. The four of them, under Eula's supervision, operated the inn and tavern successfully, though they didn't offer fishing trips anymore. After Gabriel and Martin both lost their fathers to the lake, it became off limits, as Eula adamantly refused to allow anyone, guests included, to go anywhere near the lake.

"They lived happily for many years, and in 1859, Florence gave birth to Eula's first grandchild, a pretty black-haired girl named Ina Fisher. A year later, Gabriel and Marguerite had a son and named him Theodore Juzan.

"That takes us to 1860, where our story continues...tragically."

Chapter 9

One steamy night, after all the guests had retired for the evening, Martin and Gabriel met at the tavern, as they always did, for an end-of-the-day beer. Earlier that day Martin had told Gabriel he had something to show him, and after they sat down, Martin tossed a leather-bound book across the table. It slid and stopped directly in front of Gabriel.

"What's this?" Gabriel asked, touching the cover.

"Open it and look for yourself." Martin sipped his beer.

Gabriel picked it up and looked at it. On the spine were thick black numbers reading *1841*. It was some sort of journal. He thumbed through the brittle, yellowed pages. "Where'd you get this?"

"I found it in a box in the loft above the barn. I don't know why it was hidden away up there all these years when there's so much information about the inn and tavern that we could have used. There are facts and figures that would've helped us greatly in running this place." He paused while Gabriel turned page after page. "Go to the last couple entries."

Gabriel flipped forward to the final entries, dated just before his father's death. They were written in his father's handwriting.

August 6, 1841

Leon and I learned of a bank coach carrying a trunk of gold that will be passing our lake tomorrow afternoon. We have devised a plan to intercept the coach and confiscate the gold. See the following map.

At the end of the entry were the initials *PJ*. Gabriel rubbed his thumb across them. He hadn't thought of his father in a long time, and the handwriting dredged up a melancholy feeling he wasn't familiar with. He looked at the next page and examined the sketch of the road that led around the lake and down the hill. He could clearly make out the bluff and the curve of the road. Gabriel studied the drawing for a moment and then turned the page.

August 7, 1841

Our plot did not go as planned. To the contrary, it went horribly wrong. The bank coach veered from the road at the highest point of the bluff and crashed into the lake. Leon drowned in an effort to retrieve the trunk of gold. PJ

August 8, 1841

We buried Leon today up on the bluff. I will try to retrieve the gold as soon as this passing storm breaks. PJ

August 9, 1841
The storms are still heavy, but I'm sure they will break tomorrow. PJ

There were various methods scribbled on the bottom of the page about how to fish the trunk out of the lake. Gabriel couldn't figure out which method his father had decided to use, if any. Martin sat silently and drank his beer, watching Gabriel's face as he read the journal.

Gabriel flipped to the next page, but it was blank. "Where's the rest?"

"That's it. I think August 10th was probably the day Pierre drowned in the lake, only two days after my father drowned. And now we know why."

Gabriel furrowed his brow. "It was all such a blur back then, but I seem to remember my mother saying my father died only a couple days after Leon drowned." He flipped the pages back and looked at the map again. After a moment, he looked up at Martin. "Our fathers both died for gold?" he asked, slightly shaking his head in disbelief.

Martin nodded. "According to your father's own handwriting in that very book you're holding, yes, there's gold in the lake."

Gabriel didn't respond. He simply stared at his Indian friend, trying to comprehend what he had just learned. He had never before questioned why his father was in the lake the day he drowned. Gabriel had been young at the time and hadn't given it much thought. He tried to remember that day but it was all too fuzzy. After a few moments, he asked, "Why didn't our mothers tell us about this?"

"I don't know the answer to that, but it certainly explains why my mother hates that lake so much." Martin took a drink of his beer. "Gabe, you're missing the point."

Gabriel shook his head and shrugged. "What's the point?"

"They never retrieved it."

Gabriel stared at him. "What?"

Martin lowered his voice to a whisper. "They never retrieved it. The gold is still out there."

Gabriel continued to stare at him.

Martin raised his eyebrows and grinned. "So?"

Gabriel instantly realized his lifelong friend's intention. "No, Martin, we mustn't go anywhere near the lake. Not even for this. Your mother will throw a fit."

"I'm thirty-four years old now. I'm married with my own child. My mother doesn't have a voice in what I do." He chugged the rest of the beer and placed his empty mug upside down on the table, as if to prove his point.

Gabriel closed the book and slowly pushed it across the table toward Martin. He reached for his mug and raised it to his lips.

"Gabe, do you want to spend the rest of your life taking care of other people? What about Marguerite? Doesn't she deserve better than this?" Martin waved his hands around the room.

"After just learning what happened to our fathers, how could you even suggest such a thing?" Gabriel plopped his mug on the table, sloshing some of the liquid onto the wood.

Martin sighed and leaned forward, placing his elbows on the table. "Don't you understand?" He spoke slowly. "They never retrieved the gold from the lake. It's still there." He paused, allowing the fact to sink in. "Do you know what kind of future that could mean for our business and our families? Our wives wouldn't have to work so hard. Our children would be set for life."

Gabriel leaned back and crossed his arms across his chest, shaking his head. "I don't think so. I think we should leave well enough alone. No sense in stirring up trouble. Your mother would be livid if she even heard you talking like this."

Martin raised his voice in frustration. "My mother isn't the one who does all the damn work around here. I'm tired of slaving sunup 'til sundown. We take care of the inn and the tavern, and our wives do all the cooking and cleaning and minding the children." He paused to compose himself and lowered his voice. "You know, I'd like to have more children."

Gabriel shook his head, not understanding the connection.

Martin continued, "I'd love to have a son someday, but every night, Florence is so beat, she falls into bed and is immediately asleep. She's as exhausted as I am. I don't know about your wife, but mine has had enough." He wiped beads of sweat from his brow. "And this damn heat isn't helping. This has been the hottest summer we've ever had."

"Yeah, it's been a scorcher," Gabriel added.

"Too bad we can't go for a swim. I'd go if it weren't for those cottonmouths. Damn things are taking over the lake." He pointed his finger at Gabriel as he came back to the topic at hand. "But honestly, I don't care about no snakes if I can get that gold."

"Martin, really, you should drop this. I don't need to lose you to the cottonmouths. Imagine how much work there'd be for me to do around here if something happened to you."

Martin sighed in frustration and stared down at the book on the table for a moment. He grabbed it, abruptly stood up, and marched toward the door. The sound of his boots on the wooden floor reverberated around the room.

Gabriel yelled after him, "Get some sleep, Martin. We have a busy day tomorrow. Forget about the gold."

Martin slammed the door on his way out. The glasses on the shelf behind the bar rattled against each other.

Gabriel grabbed the dirty beer mugs and rose and placed them on the bar. He had returned to the table to wipe it off when Marguerite entered. She was wearing a thin white shift and he could see right through it. She looked like a disheveled angel with her dark hair cascading around her shoulders. He seldom saw her with her hair down. In this moment, she was just as beautiful as the day he married her.

"When are you coming to bed?" she asked as she yawned.

"I'm coming right now, dear. Why are you up?"

"It's too hot." She fanned her face with her hand. "I woke up and you weren't there, so I came to check on you. I just saw Martin sulking across the yard. What's the matter with him?"

"Oh, we had a bit of a disagreement, but it's nothing." Gabriel began extinguishing the lanterns.

Marguerite stood quietly in the doorway, waiting for him.

Before he blew out the last lantern, he turned to look at her. "Are you happy here, Marguerite?"

"Of course I am. Why do you ask?"

"Martin says there's gold in the lake that would make us all rich. He wants to go after it."

"Gold in the lake? That's ridiculous. Where did he get such an idea? And does he know how upset his mother would be if he went down to the lake?"

"I know. I told him it wasn't a good idea, but he seems to have his mind made up." Gabriel didn't address the first part of her question.

"Don't allow him to do anything stupid, Gabe. That lake is dangerous. It's filled with snakes. And Eula will be furious."

"Martin is a grown man and he'll do as he wants. I'm not his father."

"No, his father drowned in the lake," she replied sarcastically.

"I know," he said as he wrapped his arm around her shoulder. "Let's go to bed."

Chapter 10

Every day for the next four scorching days, instead of tending the garden, Martin spent sunup until sundown in the rowboat trolling the lake for the trunk. Covering his gardening duties while he was otherwise occupied was none other than his wife, Florence. The heat had peaked at one hundred five degrees during the last three weeks and the nighttime temperatures were only slightly cooler. Everyone—caretakers and guests alike—complained incessantly about the hot, humid weather.

On the fifth day, as dusk fell, Martin returned from trolling and found his mother rocking little Ina to sleep on the front porch of their cottage behind the inn. She fanned the baby as she patted Ina's fat little thigh. They were both covered in a gloss of sweat.

"Where's Florence?" he asked his mother.

"I imagine she's still out in the garden. She's been tending it since early this afternoon. I don't know why she waited until the day was at its hottest to go out there, and I have no idea why she's not back yet. Where have you been running off to for the last few days?"

Martin stood on the grass and looked at his feet. He knew his mother would be furious if he told her the truth, but he was a grown man. Even so, he was still afraid of this woman and her hot Indian temper. He mumbled, "I've been down at the lake."

She stopped rocking. "Why would you be down there?"

When he didn't answer, she rose and walked inside with his baby, the wooden planks of the porch creaking with each step. He knew she would return after placing Ina in her bed so he waited, ready to face his mother's wrath. She came back out a moment later. He could see in the dimming light that her face was red with fury.

"Martin, tell me what you've been doing down there."

He took a deep breath and stood up straight. "Mother, I'm searching for that trunk of gold."

Her eyes widened, and her hands rose to her hips. Her voice grew in volume and intensity. "Where did you hear about that, and why would you want to dig up the past?"

"I'm not digging up anything, I'm just searching for an old trunk full of gold—gold that will make our lives better." He turned away from the porch and headed toward the garden to find his wife. He was hot and cranky and in no mood for this argument.

"Martin, you don't understand," she called after him. "Nothing about that gold will make our lives better. It will only cause death and destruction, heartache and pain."

He stopped and turned back. "That's nonsense, Mother. It's just metal. Metal can't do any of those things. Now, if you'll excuse me, I need to go find my wife instead of standing here arguing with you." Again, he walked away.

His mother yelled after him, "You don't know the pain it will cause, Martin!"

He grunted and waved his hand behind his head, brushing off her comment.

When he arrived at the garden, he didn't see Florence anywhere, but her gardening tools were on the ground, so he knew she wouldn't be far. Her hat and gloves were resting on a nearby tree stump at the end of one of the rows of maize.

"Florence?" he called out, but there was no answer.

He walked through the rows of maize, beans, and tomatoes, looking down each row as he passed. He called her name again and again but she didn't respond. He started moving faster, running up and down each row and cutting through the plants to the next row. His hair was soon plastered to his forehead, and a bead of perspiration dripped into his eye. The salt stung and he stopped for a moment to rub his eyes. When he opened them again, he saw her shoe under a stalk of maize. He screamed her name as he ran toward the shoe. He found her lying face down, unmoving, in a row between maize stalks. Her arms were as white as clouds. He fell to his knees and turned her over. Her skin was cool and dry. She flopped over like a ragdoll. He checked her pulse. There was none. He placed his head on her chest. He heard no heartbeat. He checked her ankles for snake bites and found none.

He cried as he picked her up and carried her back to the house.

"What happened?" his mother screamed as he neared the porch.

"I don't know," he panted. He walked up the steps and gently placed her body on the bench on the porch. "She's not breathing. Maybe it was a rattler, or maybe the heat killed her."

His mother's face turned from angry red to frightened pale. "It wasn't a snake and it wasn't the heat. You've disturbed the lake. It was the curse."

He rose and got within an inch of his mother's face. "Mother, stop your nonsense," he screamed at her.

The sleeping baby inside the house and began to cry. Eula quietly turned away and walked into the house to see after her.

Chapter 11

Following his wife's death, Martin returned to his quest for the gold with even more fervor than before. He spent every moment on the lake, trolling for the trunk. He didn't eat. He didn't sleep. His brown Indian skin had turned black under the summer sun. The high temperatures didn't let up and there had been no rain. The crops in the garden were wilted from the heat and almost dead, so there was no use tending them any longer. The woodland animals had even moved closer to the lake for relief from the drought and heat.

Martin had only spoken to his mother once since Florence died—the afternoon they buried her. He'd asked what she meant by saying it was the curse. His mother wrung her hands as she explained the incidents of twenty years ago and the curse she'd placed on the gold. Martin rolled his eyes at her and called her a superstitious old woman. He stormed out of the cottage and slammed the door. He had been sitting in the rowboat ever since.

He shook his head at his mother's story as he threw a large net onto the water, watched it sink, and then rowed feverishly in his small boat. He hoped the net would catch on the trunk and he'd be able to retrieve it. Somehow, he thought finding the trunk would justify his wife's death, so he refused to stop looking for it. He had to find it. It was his fault Florence was in the field doing his chores that day, so it was his fault she collapsed in the heat. It was his fault his young daughter was now without a mother and he without a wife. When he found the gold, his daughter would at least be set for life. His wife's death would not be in vain.

He pulled the net from the water for the fiftieth time that day. It came up freely, just as it had every time before. He folded it, pitched it out over the water again, and began rowing. His arms ached from repeating the task so many times. His skin was scorched and his tongue was dry and swollen. He kept rowing. He glanced over at the bank and saw his mother standing there watching him. He ignored her and turned his attention back to rowing. She had been standing in the same spot for days; he wished she'd go away. When he had gone about fifty feet, he tugged on the net again—nothing. He pulled it in, folded it, and tossed it out again. After it sank and he rowed another fifty feet, he pulled it in again—nothing. His stomach ached from not having eaten anything for days, but he refused to abandon his mission. He would find the trunk, or he would die trying.

When dusk fell, he pulled the net in and glanced over at the shoreline. His mother had finally gone back home and left him to his work, but he was too tired to continue. He lay back and placed his head on the rim of the boat. Perhaps if he rested his eyes for a few minutes, he'd have the energy to continue shortly.

When he opened his eyes again, night had fallen. The stars shone brightly but there was no moon, so the blackness of the sky blended with the blackness of the trees on the horizon which blended with the blackness of the water, and he couldn't see his hands in front of his face. It was still ungodly hot. He wiped sweat from his brow as a coyote howled from the shore and other coyotes around the lake joined the song.

He sat up and threw the net out again. He rowed, but didn't have any idea which way he was going, so he stopped for a moment and looked at what he thought should be the shoreline. If he could see a light at the inn or the tavern, he could get a bearing on where he was. He saw nothing but blackness. The coyotes continued their howl.

He was so hot and tired, he decided to bring in the net and sleep for a little while longer. He tugged on the net, but it wouldn't give; it was stuck on something. His heart began to race. He yanked on the net again and the boat listed to one side. It had to be the trunk.

He didn't know what to do next. He knew he couldn't allow the net to become slack. It might dislodge from the trunk and he wouldn't be able to find it again. He decided to tie it to the back of the boat and wait until the sun rose to get his bearings. He would then retrieve the trunk and his life would change forever.

He reclined and stared at the twinkling stars.

* * *

"Gabe! Gabe!" Eula shook him. "Gabe, wake up!" she called, out of breath.

He grunted and opened his eyes. "What? What is it?" he mumbled.

At the same time, Marguerite sat up. "Is something wrong with the children?"

"No," Eula whimpered, "It's Martin." Eula wiped the tears from her face.

"What's wrong with Martin?" Gabriel sat up and swung his legs from under the bed covers to the floor. "Is he still on the lake?"

"Yes, I just checked on him. His boat is anchored in the same place it was last night, but he's nowhere to be seen."

Martin stood up and grabbed his trousers from the rocking chair in the corner. "He's probably under water, diving for that stupid trunk."

"No, Gabe," she began crying. "I watched the boat and waited for a long time for him to surface, but he didn't. And the lake is like glass. He's not out there."

Marguerite walked around the bed and wrapped her arm around Eula's shoulder. "That's impossible. He's probably napping in the boat."

She shook her head. "I called for him over and over. He didn't answer."

Gabriel tucked his shirt in as he headed toward the door. If Martin's not in the water and he didn't respond to his mother's calls, something must be wrong. He felt a pang of dread rise in his chest, and he started to run the moment he exited the front door. Usually the cool mist of early morning sat on the ground and surrounded the trees, but today was clear. Today would again be as hot as the depths of Hell. The sun hadn't yet peaked over the treetops, and the temperature was already unbearable. Gabriel ran as fast as he could down the path and emerged into the clearing near the dock. He looked over the glassy lake and just as Eula said, there sat Martin's rowboat anchored in the same spot as last night.

He cupped his hands around his mouth and yelled, "Martin!" He got no response. "Martin, hang on, I'm coming," he yelled as he stepped into the second rowboat.

He untied it and rowed frantically out to Martin's boat, his oars causing the still water to ripple in an ever-expanding circle of wrinkles. After what seemed like hours of moving in slow motion, he finally reached Martin's boat. He reached out and grabbed the side of Martin's boat to pull the two vessels together. He looked inside and gagged at the sight. Martin was in his boat, lying crumpled on the floor. That's why no one could see him from the dock. He faced upwards toward the sky. His skin was pale. His lips were cracked open. His swollen tongue stuck out of his mouth. His lifeless eyes gazed on a fixed spot in the sky. Gabriel tied the boats together and then climbed into Martin's boat. He shook Martin, but he knew it was no use. His friend didn't respond. He was gone.

With tears in his eyes and dread even more present in his chest, he climbed back into his own boat and began rowing toward Eula, who waited on the shore with Marguerite's arm around her. He paddled as hard as he could but Martin's boat wouldn't move. It was as if it was stuck on something.

Gabriel crawled back into Martin's boat and found a taut fishing net tied to the back and hanging into the water. He grabbed a handful of the net and pulled. It wouldn't budge.

"I'll be damned," he whispered to himself. "He found it."

Gabriel looked to his left and right, drawing an imaginary line from the largest moss-draped oak on the north shore to a group of three pines on the south shore. Then he looked to the east. A cropping of large rocks sat on the bluff, and to the west, the inn. When he was certain he had mentally marked the spot, he released the net and allowed it to sink.

He then rowed Martin's body to his waiting mother.

Chapter 12

Following the horrible death of her son, Eula suddenly looked older than her fifty-five years. Dark circles surrounded her puffy eyes, which were swollen from shedding too many tears. Her posture seemed to have caved in as her shoulders slumped. Years ago, she had lost her husband to the gold and now her only child.

Following Martin's funeral, Eula sat alone on the banks of Lake Juzan for three days and three nights straight, staring into the black water. She refused to speak with anyone, telling Marguerite and Gabriel to leave her alone to grieve. On the third evening, Marguerite couldn't stand it anymore. She walked down to the lake and tried to console Eula, but Eula wouldn't speak to her. She wouldn't speak to anyone. Marguerite sat next to her on the sand and prodded her gently.

"Eula, sometimes bad things just happen. There's nothing you can do about Martin's death."

Eula stared straight ahead at the lake and quietly said, "But I'm the one who placed the curse."

"Curse? What curse?"

Eula stared straight ahead and didn't respond. Her eyes were bloodshot and tears trickled out onto her wrinkles. Sadness radiated from every line in her face.

"What curse, Eula?" Marguerite repeated softly.

Eula sighed and looked down at the sand. "Almost twenty years ago, my dear Leon drowned trying to retrieve a trunk of gold from the bottom of this lake."

"So there really is gold in the lake?"

Eula nodded solemnly.

"I thought Gabe was just telling me an old wife's tale."

"No, dear, there really is gold down there. My husband died for it."

"What about this curse?"

Eula looked at Marguerite and frowned. "When I found out Pierre didn't try to save my husband, that he was more interested in the gold than in those he loved, I became so enraged, I..." She dropped her head and her shoulders slumped.

Marguerite watched her, not knowing what to say to get her to continue.

After a few moments, Eula said, "I...I placed a curse on the gold. Anyone who goes after it will die a horrible death." She looked back up at Marguerite with deep sorrow in her eyes.

Marguerite stared at her. She was speechless.

When Marguerite didn't respond, Eula continued. "I was so angry with Pierre for being so cold and callused. At the time, I could have never imagined my own son would die because of my anger. I never dreamed in a million years my rage would take the life of my only child."

Marguerite sat quietly next to her. She expected Eula to break down and weep, but it didn't happen. Eula remained stoic as she gazed at the lake.

That evening, after Marguerite put the children to bed, she and Gabriel relaxed in their living room. He read the paper while she darned some stockings.

"Gabe, I'm really worried about Eula."

"I know. I am, too. She's absolutely devastated. I don't really know how to help her."

"It's not only grief. She told me that the gold in the lake is real." Marguerite paused, wondering how much she should tell Gabriel about his father's feud with Eula.

Gabriel folded the newspaper, placed it on the side table, and looked at Marguerite over the rim of his reading glasses. "She told you it's real?"

Marguerite nodded, knowing she needed to tell him the whole truth. "She told me something else, too. Something disturbing. She said when her husband drowned, she was so upset at your father for not trying to save him, she placed a curse on the gold. She did it in anger and revenge, and she thinks her curse is dangerous to anyone who goes searching for the gold."

"A curse." Gabriel said, more as a statement, not a question.

"That's what she said." Marguerite shrugged.

"That's why she's kept us away from the lake all these years." He looked out the front window into the darkness. "Now it all makes sense. I wonder if Eula thinks my father died of her curse, and if so, has she been hiding it from me all these years?"

Marguerite left him to his thoughts for a moment, the only sound in the room being the ticking clock on the wall.

Finally breaking the silence, she said, "I don't think grief for Martin is what Eula's feeling. I think it's guilt. She's convinced that her curse killed her son and her guilt is eating at her."

"Well, if she believes that, then I can understand why she's so upset, but who really believes in curses? It was bad luck, plain and simple. This ungodly heat killed Florence and a mixture of the heat and his own heartache and stubbornness killed Martin." Gabriel shook his head. "I should have rowed out there and brought him some water, if nothing else. I feel just as guilty as Eula."

"Don't blame yourself, Gabe. We both figured he'd come in when he was ready. We decided to give him space to grieve, remember?"

"Yeah, I know. I just miss him so much."

"Me, too."

* * *

As Marguerite and Gabriel discussed Eula and her curse, a dense fog rolled in and quickly enveloped Lake Juzan. One couldn't see more than a few feet. Eula rose from the bank and slowly stepped off the shore. She paused ankle deep in the water, her boots turning from tan to dark brown as they soaked it up. She took another step forward. Her stockings became cool. Another step. The skirt of her linen dress grew heavy as it soaked up what felt like gallons and gallons of water. Another step. Her fingertips felt the coolness of the lake. Another step to her waist, then to her chest.

When the water reached her neck, she felt the pressure of it against her chest, restricting her breath.

Her garments felt as heavy as her guilt, pulling her down. Her knees felt weak, but again she stepped forward. The water rose above her chin and lapped against her lips. The fog encircled her. Even if someone came down to the shore at that very moment, they wouldn't be able to see her. She prayed for absolution from her most disastrous deed, realizing her anger at Pierre Juzan had turned on her. Creating the curse was the worst thing she had ever done, and her only son had paid the price. She took two more steps, allowing the water to cover her head and fill her lungs, hopeful that the payment of her own life would be enough to stop the curse from causing any more pain.

Chapter 13

"Gabriel, I swear if you ever go anywhere near that lake again, I will take Theodore and Ina and leave you forever," Marguerite threatened as she slammed a loaf of bread down on the table and began slicing it.

It was rare for the inn to be void of guests and for the family to share a meal alone in the tavern. With the privacy came a conversation Gabriel wasn't too keen on participating in.

He looked down at his half-empty plate of greens and potatoes and didn't say a word. He knew burying Eula was deeply upsetting for Marguerite as Eula was almost like a mother to her, so he knew she was very sensitive and emotional right now. He didn't want to spark her anger or her tears by saying the wrong thing, so he remained silent. He hadn't told her about the net hooked to Martin's boat, but he was sure he knew where the gold was and confident that he could get it. If he could avoid this conversation with her until he retrieved the trunk, he knew she would change her threats to thanks. Once she saw the gold and held it in her hands, she would forget all about taking the children and leaving him. He was going to make her a wealthy woman, beyond her wildest dreams, with servants waiting on her hand and foot instead of her waiting on everyone else.

Ignoring his wife's threat, he reached across the table and grabbed a slice of bread and took a bite. He glanced at the children as he chewed. His son, Theodore, softly snored in his bassinet next to the table. His sweet face pulled at Gabriel's heartstrings. Didn't his son deserve more in life to look forward to than running a tavern? And what about Ina? The toddler sat next to him and messily shoveled potatoes into her mouth, ignoring the adults' conversation. The child had lost both her parents and her grandparents to the quest for the gold. Wasn't she entitled to the riches it offered after her family had been decimated in the pursuit? Of course she was. The poor little thing was now an orphan. He reached over and rubbed the top of her head. She giggled and pushed his hand away and shoveled more potatoes into her mouth. He loved these children with all his heart. His mind was made up. He would go after the gold, but he wouldn't tell Marguerite until after the fact.

"Promise me you'll leave it alone, Gabe," Marguerite said as she pushed a stray strand of hair from her face and sat down across from him to finish eating.

He remained silent. He didn't know how he'd get out of a promise like that. He wondered how he could phrase a promise that wouldn't later sound like a boldfaced lie after he found the gold.

"Gabe?" she snapped.

"What?" he yelled back, startling baby

Theodore. The boy began to scream in his cradle.

"That's a good boy. Keep your mother occupied while I make you a rich man," Gabriel thought as he filled his mouth with a huge forkful of greens.

Marguerite rose, picked up the crying infant, and bounced him in her arms in an attempt to soothe him, but his wails did not stop. "We are done with this gold nonsense, Gabriel Juzan! I have to put these children to bed."

She held her hand out toward Ina and wiggled her fingers for the child to come with her. Ina jumped up from the table and grabbed Marguerite's hand.

"I'll get the dishes after I tuck the children in, and then we'll talk more about this," she called from the doorway.

Gabriel nodded as she left, but he was determined to avoid the conversation at all cost. As Marguerite entered the front door of the tavern, returning to continue the conversation, Gabriel snuck out the back door without a sound. He quickly tiptoed to the inn and made sure he was in bed and asleep before she found him.

He loved his wife, and he didn't want to lie to her.

Chapter 14

The following day, while Marguerite busied herself preparing rooms for anticipated guests, cleaning, cooking, and caring for Theodore and Ina, Gabriel snuck down to the lake and rowed out to the spot where he was certain he had left the net. He looked to the right and left—oak, pines. He looked in front and behind—rocks on the bluff, inn. Perfect!

Strangely, the water looked bottomless and black to him. It was usually a murky brown color. He looked up at the cloudless sky and didn't see any difference from any other day. He shrugged to himself as he looked back at the black water.

He glanced back toward the shore one more time to make sure Marguerite hadn't followed him. But what if she had? It wasn't like he could hide in a rowboat in the middle of the lake. But if she caught him, she would be furious, and he really didn't want to attract her wrath. She was a mean woman when she was cross. He chuckled. Well, she'd get over it once she ran her fingers through the gold in the trunk. He smiled at the thought. They were going to be very, very rich, and she couldn't possibly be annoyed with him for that.

He dropped the anchor over the side and let out the rope. He released more and more of the rope and was almost at the end of the line when it finally went slack and he knew it rested on the bottom. "Gee," he mumbled to himself, "that's a thirty-foot rope." He knew the lake was deep in spots, but it had never before occurred to him until that moment *how* deep it was. "No wonder no one's been able to retrieve the trunk before."

Suspecting the trunk would be too heavy to lift to the surface by sheer manpower, he had recalled the ideas written in his father's journal on ways to raise the trunk, and he had brought two extra ropes with him. The plan was to dive down and tie both ropes around the trunk, and then hoist it up into the boat. He hoped he could do so without capsizing the small vessel because it'd be a long swim back to the shore. There were dangerous snakes in these waters, and one wouldn't want to stay in there any longer than necessary. He tied the ends of the two ropes to the boat and then slapped the water with his paddle to scare off any snakes that might be lurking. He glanced again at the shore, just in case his wife appeared. The coast was clear. He grabbed the loose ends of both ropes and dove into the black depths.

It had been so hot the whole summer, the cool water felt refreshing. Down, down, down he went. His ears popped with the pressure. He felt around in the blackness, hoping to find the edge of the net floating in the water. He felt nothing. When his lungs felt as if they would burst, he returned to the surface. He looked around again at the landmarks to make sure he was in the crosshairs of the oak, the pines, the rocks, and the inn. Yes, the trunk had to be right here.

He took another deep breath and dove again. About half way down, he felt something brush his thigh. He figured it was one of the ropes, then realized it might be the net. Adrenaline pumped through his veins in anticipation. He grabbed in the direction where he felt the object, but nothing was there. He froze for a moment as an alarming thought came to mind. What if it had been a snake? The snakes around here could kill a man with one bite. It would be a horrific and painful death. He ignored the thought and kept swimming downward, trying not to be too disappointed that he hadn't found the net yet.

When he reached the bottom, his ears pounded from the pressure. He could feel it in his jaw and across his whole head. He quickly groped around in the blackness, knowing he wouldn't be able to stay down too long. There was nothing but weeds and silt. He kicked off the bottom and shot up again to the surface. He took a deep breath and turned to check the landmarks once again. When he turned to look behind him, he came face to face with the most dreaded of snakes—the cottonmouth. Its snout was not more than a foot from his face, and Gabriel saw its tail flicker in the water nearly three feet away. It was huge, solid black except for tan markings on its face. Gabriel remained as still as possible, hoping the creature was as startled as he and would turn and swim away.

The snake quickly slithered across the surface of the water, but it didn't swim in the opposite direction. It darted directly at him and struck him on the cheek. He cried out as the serpent dashed away, disappearing as fast as lightning.

Gabriel's right cheek throbbed with an agonizing pain that felt like fire. He had never felt anything like this before. He pulled himself back into the boat and stood up, looking wildly around at the shore to see if anyone was nearby to help him. As he scanned the banks, the vision in his right eye suddenly seemed as if a cotton gauze had covered it. It remained fuzzy for a few moments, then went black. He held his hand in front of his face and couldn't see it with his right eye. He wondered if the snake had put his eye out or if the poison was moving so quickly that it had already taken his vision. No, he could see just a moment ago. It must be the poison. Oh my gawd! How fast does this poison travel? He placed his hand on his cheek. It was on fire.

He know he would die if he didn't get to shore and get help. He grabbed the rope that held the anchor. The whole right side of his head, neck, and shoulder screamed in pain. The poison was moving through his body at an alarming rate. He sat down and let go of the rope as he clutched his right shoulder with his left hand. He looked again toward the shore and the inn. His right eardrum felt as if it was going to explode. He wailed loudly, but in the middle of his cry, his voice came out in a squeak as his throat began to swell shut. He clawed at his neck. Breath wouldn't come. He instantly realized he was going to die alone in the middle of the lake. Marguerite would never forgive him. His chest constricted and he collapsed in the boat, clutching his throat as he tried to catch his next breath. He felt the poison making his heart jump. He dropped his hand from his throat to his chest and could feel his heart pounding. He fell backward onto the floor of the boat and gazed up at the clear, blue sky. In his final moments, a sense of calm came over him as he realized death would be better than this agony that ripped through his body.

Within a few short minutes, he was gone.

Strangely, the curse never crossed his mind.

Chapter 15

After spending an hour walking around the property searching for her husband, Marguerite reluctantly walked down to the lake. She hoped she wouldn't find him there, but she knew her stubborn husband would go after that gold. Even though she'd threatened him with leaving, in her heart, she knew her threats were empty. She could never make good on her promise to leave. She loved him more than life itself, and where would she go? A woman with two small children would have an extremely difficult time surviving without a husband. As she walked through the pines, she thought of Eula and Martin and Florence. Her thoughts expanded to Gabriel and Martin's fathers. She was overwhelmed with sadness that so many had lost their lives in the quest for the gold. Even if her husband found the trunk and they became rich, how could she celebrate after such loss and tragedy? It would be appalling to rejoice over something that had killed so many.

She emerged into the clearing, and when she

reached the sandy shore, she froze in her tracks. One of their rowboats sat in the middle of the lake, its occupant unseen. She was furious at her husband. She didn't see him and figured he was diving for the trunk, so she waited for him to surface. She raised her hand to her brow to shield her eyes from the sun and its reflection on the black, swampy water, and she watched the bobbing craft for a few moments. When Gabriel didn't resurface, she untied the second boat and rowed out there. In the five minutes it took her to reach Gabriel's boat, she knew something was horribly wrong as he hadn't surfaced, but she was not prepared for the sight she encountered.

Her husband lay on the floor of his boat, eyes opened and lifeless. His right eye was colorless, a grayish-white pupil gazing up at the heavens. There were two puncture wounds on his right cheek. She knew those wounds, and it must have been a huge snake, for the marks were at least three inches apart. She nervously glanced around the lake and in Gabriel's boat.

When she was satisfied the snake was not nearby, she tied the boats together, pulled up her husband's anchor, and rowed back to shore. She didn't know how she would get his body out of the boat, and she painfully decided she'd have to wait until evening customers arrived to help. She left his body in the boat in the hot sun all day while she tended the children. Her heart felt as if it would crumble, but the wait gave her plenty of time to decide what to do next.

Her customers graciously agreed to help her bury her husband, and the next morning, they dug a grave and carefully lowered Gabriel's body into it. After they covered it, not one of them asked for breakfast.

They all understood the tavern would be closed for the day.

Within an hour of the funeral, all the guests departed, and Marguerite hung a CLOSED sign on the front door. She then packed every belonging she could fit into a wagon, gathered the children, and drove away from Lake Juzan and the curse that had claimed so many lives in her family. She headed west up the bluff. When she reached the top, she stopped and looked back over the lake. The afternoon sun danced across the smooth surface. Only the slightest ripples could be seen near the shores as birds walked along the edge picking for bugs. The pine trees on the far banks reflected on the water and a few white puffy clouds floated by, painting the sky and replicating themselves on the lake. It was serene and beautiful, or so she had always thought. She shed a single tear. She would not miss one moment of the pain that had held her family in its grips for the entire summer. If there was indeed a curse that was two generations old, Marguerite knew only one thing for sure. She needed to take Theodore and Ina as far away from the lake as possible and make them promise to never, ever return—no matter what. Marguerite clicked her tongue at the horses, and she and the children rode away from Lake Juzan.

Over the next month, she drove the wagon west as far as they could possibly go. The road finally ended at the great Mississippi River, in a town called Vicksburg.

Part III: The Best Man I've Ever Known

"Everything didn't go as smoothly as Marguerite had hoped, as the country soon after found itself in the middle of the War Between the States. Marguerite faced a great struggle keeping the children safe and fed for four long years, but somehow they survived the war, the economic depression, and the assault of Grant's army on her new town.

"When the war came to an end and Vicksburg began rebuilding, Marguerite was right in the center of the restoration. She found ways to help her neighbors as well as ways to make money, and eventually she bought an old plantation that had been decimated during the war. Over the next few years, she traded and bartered for home improvements, and soon, she proved herself a very competent businesswoman. She created a successful plantation in Vicksburg without the help of slaves or a husband, and she raised Theodore and Ina all by herself. Theodore grew up working on the farm, riding through the fields of cotton and tobacco, and selling their produce in town. Ina learned to run the household staff, and at one point, she managed eight ladies who cleaned and

cooked for the family."

He paused the story as he watched a tugboat drift by. The sky was filling with dark, gray clouds, and the wind rustled the leaves of the trees as the storm drew ever so near. He wondered if he would be able to finish telling the story before the storm arrived.

The boys were oblivious to the weather. They were only interested in the next part of the tale.

"So what happened to Theodore? Did he find out about the gold?" the older boy asked.

"Well, I'll tell you about Theodore Juzan. He was raised well by his mother, and he was undoubtedly the best man I've ever known. He had dark hair and emerald green eyes, just like all the Juzans. He towered at six feet four inches, but he was as gentle as a lamb. He was an honest and hardworking man with a heart of gold.

"When he was in his twenties, his mother, Marguerite, took ill with pneumonia..."

Chapter 16

On a blistering summer afternoon in 1882, Marguerite lay in the four-poster feather bed in her room on the second floor of the plantation. She was covered in a gloss of sweat as she struggled to catch her next breath. She had grown painfully thin the last few weeks and fluid had begun to fill her lungs. She was losing the battle. A tearful Theodore sat beside her bed, holding his mother's frail hand.

"Momma, can I get you anything?"

She shook her head ever so slightly, the movement barely visible to anyone who wasn't paying close attention.

Ina, with her dark eyes full of tears, sat on the other side of the bed. She held a handkerchief in front of her lips, and Theodore knew they quivered behind the cloth.

"I want you to promise me something, Theodore," Marguerite croaked, then coughed. It was more of an exhalation than a cough, for she didn't have the strength to clear her lungs.

"Of course, Mamma, what is it?" Theodore leaned in closer.

"Promise me, whatever happens and whatever you hear or learn, you will never go back to Lake Juzan. It's a bad place."

Theodore looked at Ina. He had no idea what his mother was talking about. Ina shrugged, indicating she didn't know either. Theodore wrote off the request as the railings of a dying woman.

"All right, Momma, I promise."

Through the remainder of the day, Marguerite kept muttering incomprehensible phrases about drownings and snakes and curses, but about midnight, she became gravely quiet. Theodore and Ina remained by her bedside throughout the night, listening to her rattled breathing and knowing the end was drawing near. As the rooster began its morning song, Marguerite Juzan exhaled her last breath.

Theodore and Ina sat silently at Marguerite's bedside for a long time. Slowly the tears began.

"I guess I should go into town and call on the minister," Theodore said through his tears.

"Yes, that would be the right thing to do." After a moment, she added, "What dress do you want to bury her in?"

"She always loved that lavender one with the lace neckline. How about that one?"

Ina nodded. "I'll wash and press it while you're gone."

They hugged and sadly exited the room to go prepare for the funeral.

Two days later, they held Marguerite's wake downstairs in the parlor of the plantation house and nearly two hundred people came by to pay their respects. Marguerite Juzan had been a well-respected member of the community. For twenty years, she had attended Liberty Baptist Church, even financially supporting the construction of their new building a few years ago. She attended town hall meetings where she always added her opinion to whatever the topic of the month was. She freely gifted the town with money for leveling roads and building docks. She had built her business from nothing into a thriving and successful plantation that employed many of the local townspersons. She didn't care if they were black, white, or Indian. She paid them all a fair wage. She was very loved and would be greatly missed by everyone who knew her.

Following the wake, her remains were carried in the back of a wagon pulled by a lone white horse to the back of the plantation property. Everyone in attendance followed the wagon on foot, and the procession was an impressive half mile long. She was laid to rest beside an enormous oak tree that had been on the property for hundreds of years.

The morning following the funeral, Theodore and Ina rose early and began their new lives as proprietors of a plantation, though not much of their daily agenda changed. Theodore rode through the cotton and tobacco fields, overseeing the laborers, and Ina wandered through the big house, cooking, cleaning, and overseeing the staff.

Chapter 17

Four years following Marguerite's death, Theodore met a young lady. Betty Parker was a visiting cousin of a wealthy local family. She was spending the summer at her uncle's country estate, and from the moment they met in town, Theodore and Betty were inseparable. They talked until all hours of the night, went for romantic carriage rides, and on balmy evenings, they sat on the veranda, drinking cool tea and watching the sun set over the mighty Mississippi. Though Betty's family was quite wealthy, she didn't seem to concern herself with being the belle of the manor. She was a sweet and demure young lady who seemed more interested in making Theodore happy.

As summer drew to a close, Theodore became more and more melancholy about Betty's forthcoming departure. He couldn't imagine his life would without her. His future seemed lonely and bleak without her sweet smile and lovely face to fill his days. One evening, without telling Ina, Theodore rode over to Betty's uncle's house where Betty's parents had come to collect her and take her home to Philadelphia, and he boldly asked Betty's father for his blessing. With a glowing commendation from her uncle, her father reluctantly gave his permission for the two to wed. Theodore couldn't wait to tell her, even though he hadn't yet purchased a ring for her. He excused himself from the parlor and ran directly to find her. When he found her sitting in a chair on the back porch, he ran to her, removed his hat, and fell down on one knee.

She stared at him for a moment without expression. That's when he noticed her tear-stained face.

"Why are you crying?" he asked softly, wiping the tears from her cheek with his thumb.

"I was just thinking how much I love it here and how much I'm going to miss you when I leave."

"Betty, that's why I'm here. I don't want you to leave. Will you please stay here in Vicksburg and become my wife?"

"Your wife?"

"Yes, I just spoke with your father and received his blessing. Will you marry me?"

Slowly, a smile came to her lips. She nodded and he pulled her to her feet. As he wrapped her in his arms, she began to cry again.

"Why are you crying now?"

"These are happy tears," she replied.

He smiled. "I'm glad." He bent his head down and kissed her on the lips.

* * *

Betty couldn't have been happier. She loved life on the Mississippi, and she loved Theodore Juzan. The only thing she was a little nervous about was his friend Ina. The two lived together in the big plantation house, and Betty had not summoned the nerve to ask Theodore about the relationship.

She put the unease out of her mind as she planned a grand celebration for their wedding. She and Theodore were married at Liberty Baptist Church and held their reception at Theodore's plantation. She had never seen so many people in one room, and the thought that Theodore was so well-loved by the community warmed her heart.

During her wedding planning, she had come to know the plantation's servants very well. She had become friends with a few of them and was on a first name basis with them, insisting they refer to her as Betty instead of Miss Parker. This familiarity continued following the wedding, also. She refused to be called Mrs. Juzan, even though she was very happy with the name. She only wanted to be called by her first name.

Immediately following the grand wedding, she found herself alone all day while Theodore worked in the fields or traveled into town on business. She sought out the servants for friendship and would often share lunch with them in the kitchen. She also found pleasure in helping them with the many larger cleaning projects. They chatted and laughed as they worked, and the days without Theodore passed by a lot quicker.

Over time, she began seeing the need to update the furnishings in the plantation as most were more than twenty years old. She began redecorating the big house with newly sewn curtains, freshly weaved rugs, and brand new upholstery on the settees and sofas.

Strangely, even though she sought the company

of the servants, she never became close friends with Ina. She tended to avoid the Indian woman, as she always felt inadequate in the woman's presence, almost like she didn't belong in the Juzan household. Ina had never done anything in particular. It was just a feeling. Maybe it was jealousy of the relationship between Ina and her husband. Whatever it was, she stayed out of Ina's way when she saw her in the big house. The only time they spoke was at supper.

They dined nightly in the formal dining room with all the proper silver and crystal. The supper table would consist of Ina and Theodore and Betty, and the servants would quickly serve dishes and then disappear without a word. Betty watched Theodore and Ina interact nightly at the table, but she never spoke to Theodore about their relationship. It was obvious to her they were as close as two peas in a pod, and she was worried Theodore would tell Ina if she asked. She could just picture them having a good laugh at her expense, so she kept her questions to herself. Theodore and Ina both seemed to light up when the other came into the room, and often at supper, they laughed when they told stories and reminisced about their past—a subject Betty could not participate in. She was an outsider, plain and simple. She remained quiet and pleasant at the table, but she wished Ina would go away and stop taking her husband's attention.

* * *

After a few months, Ina walked out to the field and spoke to Theodore.

Ina's brow furrowed as she spoke. "Since you've gotten married, Betty has truly become the lady of the house. She is very good to the staff and has learned so much about running the household."

"What are you getting at, Ina? I can tell when something's bothering you."

"Oh, no, no, I'm not bothered by it in the least. It's just that since she's taken over so many of the daily responsibilities, I really don't feel like I'm needed there anymore."

"Nonsense."

"No, Theodore, it's not nonsense. You need to live in your house with your wife managing your staff. I think it's time I move out and find my own home."

"The big house *is* your home."

She looked at the ground and shook her head. "No, it's *your* home. My family has always been friends and colleagues, but I am not a Juzan, and the house is not mine. I need to find another place to live."

"Are you sure that's what you want to do?"

She nodded.

"Do you want to move to town or would you like to stay here on the land?"

"I hadn't really thought about it, but I guess I don't have a choice since there's no place to live here on the land."

"Ina, I don't want you to move away. You are my family. I don't care if your last name isn't Juzan. I'll tell you what. You stay in the big house for a little while longer and I'll build you a cottage on the back of the property. It won't take too long. You can stay on the land and not have to clash with Betty over control of the servants. How's that sound?"

Ina's face radiated with happiness. "Oh, Theodore, I knew you'd come up with a solution!" She gave him a great big hug and ran back toward the house.

Theodore halted all other work on the farm while the workers built a quaint cottage for Ina. It was made from hewn planks and covered with cyprus shingles and painted shutters. Ina loved it.

After the cottage was finished and Ina had moved in, she searched to find projects to occupy her time. She didn't know how ladies of leisure survived the boredom. She spent more time in town shopping and dining. She tried to find a group to join, but the only one she found was the ladies auxiliary at church who met on Wednesday mornings to quilt and gossip. Even though the ladies were nice enough, it was not her cup of tea, and she never went back after the first time. She was also lonely living all by herself, so she snuck out a few times and went to the saloon in town. She always felt a pang of guilt for days after doing something so mischievous, but she was growing more and more stir-crazy. She found she occupied most of her time dressing for supper and walking up to the big house to join Theodore and Betty in the formal dining room. She could tell by Betty demeanor that the woman was happy to have Ina out of her house, but she didn't hold it against her. After all, and man and wife needed their privacy. She wondered if she would ever find a man of her own to marry.

One evening at supper, Theodore tapped his knife on the rim of his wineglass and claimed he had an announcement to make.

"Ina, I'm happy to announce that Betty is pregnant. We're expecting our first child." His smile broadened as he eagerly awaited his lifelong friend's congratulations.

Ina looked back and forth between Theodore and Betty. "I'm so happy for you both. Betty, you'll be a great mother, and Theodore, I know how caring and loving you are. You'll be the best father the Juzan family has ever known."

The three had a happy celebration for the coming child.

A few weeks later, Theodore saw Ina walking across the field. The sight certainly wasn't unusual, for she often walked from her cottage to the big house, but this morning she was walking directly toward Theodore. He watched her approach from atop his horse, where he was overseeing the corn planting.

"Theodore, can you take a break from what you're doing? I need to speak with you about something important." Her brow was furrowed.

The last time he saw that furrowed brow, she had moved out. He wondered what news she would have for him this time. "Of course I can."

He ordered the workers to continue and climbed down from his steed. The two strolled across the field toward the giant oak tree where Marguerite was buried. When they sat in the shade, Theodore removed his hat and wiped the sweat from his brow with a handkerchief.

Ina kept her eyes straight ahead on the field. "Theodore, I have some disturbing news. I don't know how to tell you this, and I don't know what to do." Her eyes filled with tears.

"What is it? Nothing can be that bad." He started to put his handkerchief back in his pocket, then decided to hang onto it in case her tears spilled down her cheeks.

She looked at him, wringing her hands in her lap. For a moment he thought she was going to clam up, but then she blurted out, "I'm pregnant." She buried her face in her hands and wept.

He didn't know what to say. He sat holding the handkerchief and didn't move. She obviously was not happy about this event, and he wasn't sure if it would be appropriate to ask her who the father was. He wrapped his arm around her shoulder and decided to remain silent until she had composed herself. When her sobs finally subsided, she volunteered the information. "It was an Indian boy in town. I don't love him. It was just stupid."

"Do you want to marry him?"

"What? Marry? No, I don't want to marry him, but what am I supposed to do?"

"You'll do nothing. You'll stay right here and raise your child with mine. We've always been family and we will remain so." He smiled warmly at her. "Imagine our children growing up together the same way we did."

Ina took the handkerchief from his hand and wiped her eyes. "Really? You don't think bad of me having a child out of wedlock?"

"Bad of you? No, of course not. Why don't you come to the house for supper tonight and we'll tell Betty the news. I'm sure she'll be as excited about two babies as I am. We've been living like old folks for long enough. It'll be fun to have little ones running around the plantation."

Ina smiled weakly and nodded. After they rose, she handed him back his handkerchief and he gave her a long hug.

Chapter 18

That evening, Theodore, Betty, and Ina supped on a wild turkey Theodore had shot earlier in the day. They laughed and chatted through the entire meal, and when they had finished eating, Theodore said, "Betty, Ina has some news to tell you."

Betty raised her eyebrows toward Ina and waited.

Ina dabbed the corners of her mouth with her napkin and then placed it on the table. "Well, I'm afraid I've found myself pregnant," she blurted out.

Betty's eyes grew large, her face grew pale, and she looked back and forth between Theodore and Ina. Ina could read her expression. Betty had never said as much, but Ina knew the close relationship between Theodore and Ina had always made Betty wonder how close the two really were. She had probably jumped to the conclusion that the baby was Theodore's, though she was too much of a lady to voice her concerns. Theodore didn't take notice of the tension in his wife.

Ina quickly spoke up. "I had relations with a

boy in town, but I don't want to marry him."

Betty exhaled and her shoulders relaxed.

Ina continued, "I was pretty upset about it until Theodore said our children will grow up as siblings." She looked at Theodore and grinned. "Just like we did."

Theodore reached over, covered Ina's hand with his own, and they beamed at each other. He then turned to Betty. "So, what do you think, dear? Our little one will have a lifelong friend and playmate. Isn't that wonderful?"

"Yes, that certainly is wonderful." Betty turned to Ina and politely said, "You should consider moving back into the big house, dear. You shouldn't be alone way out there in the cottage. What if something should happen? What if the baby should decide to come early?"

Ina frowned. "No, no, I couldn't do that. I love my little cottage, and while I appreciate the offer and your concern, Betty, I'd really like to stay in my own home."

She saw a wave of relief wash over Betty's face.

Following supper, Theodore hooked up the wagon and drove Ina back to her cottage. She insisted she could walk through the field as she always did, but he wouldn't hear of it.

When they arrived at the cottage, Ina climbed down and looked up at Theodore. "I can't thank you enough for taking care of me and accepting this baby."

"Ina, we're family and I'd do nothing less. I love you and I will love your child like he or she is my own."

She gave him a warm smile and bid him a good night.

Chapter 19

On the evening of May 11, 1890, Ina gave birth to a baby boy and named him Luke Matthew Fisher. The very next morning, Betty gave birth to a baby girl and named her Penelope Marguerite Juzan. As the days and weeks passed, Betty decided she wanted to spend more time with her infant daughter and less time with the servants, so she asked Ina to resume her position in charge of the household. Each day Ina walked to the big house with Luke wrapped around her chest in a shawl. Even though the babies lived in different houses, they spent every day together, and as they grew into toddlers, they filled the big house with laughter and childlike happiness.

Each evening, the supper table was filled with their playful antics, and Theodore's smile radiated throughout the plantation. Ina had never seen him so happy. When he wasn't working, he would be found playing with the children. Betty loved seeing her husband's smile, and Ina loved being back at work. Everyone was happy and the old plantation house was, for the very first time, full of life.

As years passed, Betty became concerned that she had not conceived again. She carefully broached the subject one evening while lying in bed with Theodore.

"How do you feel about Luke?" she asked as she stared into the darkness at the shadows on the ceiling.

"What do you mean, how do I feel about him? I love that boy as if he were my own son."

"I know you do, but wouldn't you like to have your own son?"

"Well, Betty, it's not that we haven't tried. It just doesn't seem to be in the cards for us. Don't worry yourself over it. We'll teach the running of the plantation to Penny and Luke. They're both bright children and we'll be well cared for in our old age."

Betty didn't respond. She knew he was right, and if the Good Lord didn't see fit in gifting her with a son, then there wasn't much she could do about it, but it still felt like Ina had given him the son she couldn't give him.

"I'll tell you one thing about our daughter, though." He chuckled. "Her green Juzan eyes are going to help her get anything she wants in life. No one on the plantation can say no to that little girl. She's going to be quite a looker."

"Yes, she is quite beautiful," Betty said as she rolled over and faced the window. The night breeze fluttered the sheer curtains.

Theodore rolled over in the opposite direction. "Good night, dear," he said.

"Good night," Betty whispered.

As she heard her husband's soft snores, her eyes filled with tears and she cried herself to sleep.

Chapter 20

The year Penny and Luke both turned nine years old, they spent the entire summer playing in the attic. They built forts and created make-believe stores and houses, stacking trunks and boxes for walls, and hanging Betty's good sheets from the rafters.

"Luke, help me drag this trunk over there to use as a table in our store," Penny said one day.

Luke ran to her side and grabbed the handle on the other side of the trunk.

"One, two, three," Luke counted, and they pulled.

The heavy trunk moved only an inch or so, then toppled over. The lid flipped open and a dozen or more thick journals tumbled out of it.

"What are these?" Luke asked, picking up a book and flipping it open.

Penny picked one up as well and thumbed through it. "The name in this one says Pierre Juzan. That must be my grandfather or great-grandfather." She snapped the book shut. "We can sell them in our store!"

"Good idea," said Luke with a grin.

The children gathered the books and placed them on shelves in their pretend store.

As summer faded to fall, the last day before school started again, the children were again playing in the attic. That evening, Betty scolded them—as she often did—for losing track of time and not being at the table promptly for supper.

"You're late again," barked Betty as the children ran into the room and hustled into their seats at the table. The adults had already been served.

"What are you two doing up there anyway?" asked Theodore as he spread jam across the top of an opened biscuit.

"We have a pretend bookstore." Penny smiled, displaying her two missing teeth in the front.

"Well, you two should put as much energy into your schoolbooks as you do into your pretend books," Betty chastised.

"Oh, the books aren't pretend," replied Penny.

"You have real books upstairs?" asked Theodore.

Penny nodded with enthusiasm. "Yes, we found them in a trunk. They belonged to somebody named Pierre Juzan."

Theodore and Ina glanced at each other across the table. Betty watched the interaction.

"Do you know who that is, Daddy?"

Theodore cleared his throat. "Um, yes, Pierre Juzan was my grandfather. I didn't know there were any books up there."

"Oh, yes. There's a whole trunk full of them. They're some kind of journals."

"There's more than a dozen, sir," Luke chimed in. "They look like inventory from some kind of store or something."

Theodore took a sip of his iced tea. "My grandfather owned an inn and a tavern." He looked at Ina and she nodded for him to continue. "Luke, your great-grandfather was the caretaker of that inn. They were business partners for a long time."

"What happened to the inn and why are the journals here now?" asked Luke.

Ina stepped in. "Oh, that's a long story for another day. You children eat your supper so you can get cleaned up and into bed. The first day of school comes bright and early in the morning."

The rest of the meal was fairly quiet with the occasional mention of plantation business.

* * *

After Ina and Luke went home and Penny was tucked into bed, Theodore climbed the stairs to the attic to examine the journals for himself.

Chapter 21

It took Theodore three trips to cart all the books down to his office, and he spread them out across his desk. There were sixteen in all, each with the year written in bold black numbers across its spine. He lined them up—1826 to 1841—and opened the first one. It contained inventory lists, shopping lists, customer information for the inn, receipts for the tavern, and all the recipes for meals served and liquor made in the stills. All of the entries were in the same handwriting and each page was signed *PJ* at the bottom. Theodore knew this stood for Pierre Juzan. Some entries were labeled as *Reported by Leon Fisher,* but those were still in Pierre's handwriting and still contained the standard *PJ* at the bottom of the page. Theodore figured either Leon Fisher couldn't read and write or he wasn't allowed to touch the books. Either way, the records showed the two business partners made a lot of money.

He scanned the pages of the next seven books, noticing that most of the money went back into the business, but about 1833, the two started paying themselves a salary. Pierre took quite a larger sum than Leon, and as the years passed, the difference in their pay grew even more obvious. By 1840, Pierre's salary had increased by nearly two hundred percent, while Leon's had only increased by mere pennies.

Theodore saw evidence that his grandfather was not only a very successful businessman, but an exorbitantly greedy one. He wondered why Leon stayed around and tolerated such treatment. The only reason he could come up with was that Leon Fisher was an Indian and it was the 1830s.

In 1830, the Indians signed a treaty with the United States government called the Treaty of Dancing Rabbit Creek. Pierre Juzan was one of the half-breeds who signed the treaty, accepting in return a large chunk of land for himself. The full-blooded Indians could petition the government for a piece of land, but the government made it extremely difficult for them to get through the paperwork, considering most Indians didn't read or write English. The thought made Theodore realize that Leon probably didn't read or write.

The Indians barely eked out an existence as it was, so when they found how impossible it was to obtain their own land to farm on, most of them gave up the struggle and moved to the Oklahoma Territory. The ones who stayed on their native land settled for scraps. Leon was one of the ones who stayed. He had been helping Pierre build a successful business for years and obviously didn't relocate to Oklahoma as he had a wife and a young child to support. Having no parents or siblings and nowhere else to go, he was forced to accept the treatment he received from Pierre.

Theodore bookmarked the page, placed the

book down on the desk, and rose from his chair. He walked to the window and stared out into the night. He hoped he was treating Ina better than Pierre treated Leon, and after a few moments of contemplation, he decided he was. Ina was like his sister. He would never treat her unfairly. He walked back to his desk and opened the next book, and the next. They all contained pretty much the same information.

The very last journal, dated 1841, began the same as the others—inventory, supplies, receipts—but a few pages in, everything changed. The lists were replaced by a map of a road around the lake and a story about a bank coach that was coming through. Theodore flipped the pages forward and found the story continued for a few pages. It was growing quite late—well after three in the morning—but he knew he wouldn't be able to sleep until he read the story, so he settled into his big easy chair in the corner of his office, lit the oil lamp on the side table, and began reading.

According to the story, Pierre and Leon were tending bar on an extremely slow night and talked to a drunkard who'd been hired to guard a bank coach. Pierre and Leon planned a heist to steal the gold. The next entry told of the disaster of the coach and its cargo rolling off the bluff and sinking into the lake, and of Leon's untimely death while trying to save the trunk of gold. The third entry seemed to meander through ways to retrieve the trunk, though it never concluded with a definite plan of action. Theodore pause his reading and gave the situation some thought. He concluded a trunk of gold must be very heavy, so if he were Pierre, he would row out with long ropes to fish the trunk out of the lake.

Theodore looked back down at the book and turned the next page. There was nothing written on it. He flipped back and thumbed forward through the next few pages but found the story had abruptly ended. Nothing but blank pages stared back at him.

He rose and walked over to the window again. The sky had begun to turn pink on the horizon. He thought to himself, *"Since the journal ended, Pierre never got the gold. I'll be damned. Poor guy. I remember hearing he drowned in the lake. I bet the gold was the reason why."* He placed his hand on the side of the window frame and leaned against it. *"My father died on the lake, too. He died in '61 when I was just a baby. My mother struggled for two decades to build this plantation. She definitely didn't have the gold or she wouldn't have worked so hard."* He narrowed his eyes as he thought. *"Ina's family is all dead except for her and Luke, and they certainly don't have the gold."* He drummed his fingers on the windowsill and then concluded out loud, "They never retrieved it. The gold is still in the lake."

Since he had promised his mother on her deathbed he would never go near Lake Juzan, he needed to come up with another way to get the gold. After a few moments, he realized he had only one choice. He sent word for his most trusted employee to join him at the plantation house for breakfast.

Chapter 22

Carter Stuckey, a robust man who resembled jolly Father Christmas more than a strict foreman of a plantation, knocked on the front door. Ina answered.

"Oh, Mr. Stuckey! A very good morning to you, sir." She smiled at him and opened the door wide for him to enter.

"Good morning, Miss Fisher. You look lovely this morning." He removed his hat and stepped into the house.

She smoothed down her apron with her palm as she blushed. "Thank you, Mr. Stuckey. You are such a sweet talker."

"I only tell the truth, ma'am." He grinned through his long white beard. "Mr. Juzan has cordially invited me to dine with him this morning."

"Yes, he informed me you would be coming by, so I made your coffee extra strong, just the way you like it. Mr. Juzan is upstairs in his office and asked that you meet him there to discuss some business. I'll bring in your breakfast right away."

Stuckey pouted. "Oh, I knew it would be business, not a social invitation."

"You know Mr. Juzan. It's always business." Ina smiled as she closed the front door. She held her palm out in the direction of the stairway. "It's the second door on your right at the top of the stairs."

Carter nodded and carefully climbed the massive staircase. He called back down, "Thank you, Miss Fisher."

She called back up, "You're welcome, Mr. Stuckey."

He tapped lightly on the door and awaited a response. When he heard Theodore bellow, "Come in," he entered the office, and Theodore rose to greet him. The two shook hands and didn't waste any time getting down to business.

"Carter, I need you to do something for me, and you're the only one I trust with this task. I need you to go out to Lake Juzan and get some men to pull up a trunk that's on the bottom of the lake."

"A trunk? How did it get to the bottom of the lake?"

"Well, that's quite a long story I won't bore you with, but I will say it's been down there between forty and sixty years, so it may be covered with weeds and perhaps difficult to find."

"That'll be no problem, Mr. Juzan. I know men who can find a needle in a haystack. I'm sure finding a trunk in a small lake won't be too difficult. So, what would you like me to do with this trunk when I retrieve it?"

"Bring it back here. I'll reward your deed with a handsome retirement."

"Retirement? That sounds like the best offer

I've had all day!" Carter chuckled.

"Well, you bring me that trunk and it's yours."

"Consider it done."

Ina rapped lightly on the door and entered the room carrying a large tray of biscuits, honey, jam, and hot coffee. A younger girl followed with a tray of sugar ham and fried eggs. They placed the trays on the desk, and Ina poured coffee for the men before she left the room.

Carter and Theodore enjoyed a quick breakfast before Carter rose and said, "Well, I'd better get on my way to Lake Juzan if I'm ever going to retire." He laughed and pulled out a pipe and some tobacco. "I'll fill this and enjoy it on my journey."

"Is that the pipe I gave you last Christmas?"

Carter held it up so Theodore could see the carving on the side that read STUCKEY . "Yes, sir, it is. It's the best gift I've ever received."

"Well, I'll get you a matching lighter for your retirement."

"That's very nice of you, sir." He pulled his tobacco out of his pocket. "I'll be on my way and return very soon with your trunk."

Theodore bid Carter a farewell. "Notify me the moment you find it."

"I certainly will. I'll send a messenger to let you know."

They shook hands again and Carter headed toward the door.

"Oh, and Carter..." Theodore called after him.

Carter stopped and looked back at the desk, hand resting on the doorknob.

"Thanks for not asking me what's in the trunk."

Carter smiled. "I figured if you wanted me to know, Mr. Juzan, you would have told me."

Theodore nodded at him as Carter turned and walked out the door.

Chapter 23

Each day following Carter's departure, Theodore kept his eyes toward the road. He watched it like a hawk, hoping for a messenger to appear and tell him the trunk had been found. With each passing day, he grew more and more agitated that he hadn't received any word.

* * *

Penny knew something was bothering her father as she noticed his building irritation and the fact that lately his face was redder than normal. He had snapped at her on more than one occasion over the last few weeks, which was unlike him, so she made every effort to stay out of his way.

One afternoon, she passed his office door and found it ajar. Out of curiosity, she peeked in and found him writing in one of the journals that she and Luke had found in the attic. He was scribbling furiously and she didn't want to interrupt him and entice his wrath, so she slowly backed away from the door and left him alone.

That evening she readied herself for bed and wanted to say good night to her father. She approached his office door and listened. It was silent. She took a deep breath and softly knocked.

"Daddy?" she called out as she cracked open the door.

"Yes?" he replied sharply without looking up from the book on his desk.

"Is something wrong?" she asked in the sweetest voice she could muster.

"No, sweetheart, nothing is wrong. You run off the bed now, all right?"

"All right, Daddy." She ran to his desk and kissed him on the cheek. He distractedly patted her on the head.

She tiptoed from the office, pulled the door closed all but an inch, and gazed at her father for a moment. Something was definitely wrong. She hoped he would fix it very soon.

A few days later, she heard Ina in the front doorway, speaking to a messenger. The messenger stated it was imperative Mr. Juzan receive something immediately, and Ina promised to deliver it to Mr. Juzan right away. After Ina closed the front door, Penny approached her and noticed a wrinkled piece of paper in her hand.

"What's that?" Penny asked.

"It's a letter for your father."

"I'll take that up to Daddy, if you wish," Penny offered, her hand outstretched to Ina.

"All right, child, run it straight up. Don't dilly-dally."

"I won't." She grabbed the letter and bounced up the stairs, her pigtails bobbing with each step. She stopped outside her father's office door and listened. It was quiet. She looked down at the paper in her hand. She hoped the letter would make her daddy feel better. She flipped over and examined it. It was nothing special, just a folded piece of creased and dirty paper that read PIERRE JUZAN—URGENT on the front. She knocked sharply on her father's office door and heard him say, "Come in."

She approached the desk with her arm extended. "Daddy, a messenger delivered this letter for you. He said it was...imper...impera...something."

"Imperative?" He chuckled.

She smiled and her green eyes lit up. "Yes, that's what he said." It was the first time she had heard her father laugh in months.

He jumped up from his desk and met her halfway across the room.

"Ah, just what I've been waiting for." He took the letter with one hand and patted her on the head with the other. "You run along now. I have work to do." He turned his back toward her as if he had forgotten she was even standing there.

She pouted as she backed out of the room. She pulled the door closed but left it just a little ajar so she could watch him read the letter. He sat behind his desk, put his glasses on, and unfolded the letter. She kept her eyes on his face as he read the contents. He slapped his hand on the desktop and yelled, "Aha!" She jumped, startled by the noise, and softly closed the door all the way.

That evening, Penny, Betty, Luke, and Ina sat at

the dining room table awaiting the arrival of Penny's father so they could begin supper. It was not like him to be late. Penny's mother fidgeted and rearranged her table setting a dozen times. Finally she said, "Penny, run up and tell your father to come down for supper. He has worked long enough for today."

"Yes, Momma." Penny placed her napkin on the table and bolted out of the dining room and through the parlor. She took the stairs two at a time.

She knocked on his office door but he didn't respond. She knocked a second time. No answer. She turned the doorknob and inched the door open. "Daddy? Are you here?" She didn't understand what she saw. Her father was in the same position she had left him in hours ago—spectacles on, holding the letter from the messenger—except his head was on the desk and he was ghostly pale. "Daddy?" She tiptoed toward him. He didn't move. Perhaps he was asleep. She reached up and wiggled his arm. "Daddy?" His hand fell from the desk and swung like a pendulum.

"Daddy!" she screamed.

Chapter 24

Betty proved herself a fine businesswoman in her husband's stead, and the next four years on the plantation were fruitful ones. The weather cooperated, the crops were enormous, and Betty took the family business to new heights with the help of young Luke who was quickly learning the skills to be the overseer.

Sadly, Ina passed away of heart problems in 1905. She died peacefully in her bed in her quaint cottage surrounded by those who loved her—Betty, Penny, and Luke. They buried her by the giant oak tree near Marguerite and Theodore. Penny didn't see much of Luke following his mother's death. He kept to himself, living alone in his mother's cottage and burying himself in his work. She occasionally caught a glimpse of him in the fields on his horse. She admired how reliable he was when it came to running the plantation, but she sorely missed the friendship they had shared growing up. When she saw him, she always waved to him but he never waved back, and they seldom spoke as he never came to the house for supper anymore.

Since it was just Betty and Penny alone in the big house, Betty closed off most of the rooms and let the entire house staff go. Penny routinely made supper, which often consisted of only tomato sandwiches, but that was fine by her and her mother.

In 1910, Betty contracted pneumonia and didn't live more than a week after she was diagnosed. She died at the young age of forty-five. Luke and Penny buried her on the back of the property near the giant oak, in the company of Marguerite, Theodore, and Ina. Toward the end of the funeral, the sky darkened, and the clouds began a depressing drizzle with the promise of a bigger storm to come.

After the minister left, Luke carted Penny back to the big house in the wagon. By the time they arrived, thunder and pelting rain surrounded them.

"Luke, I've missed you so much the last couple years. I wonder if you'll consider moving back into the big house with me," Penny asked softly as they rode across the field.

He didn't say anything for a long time, but then surprised her with a positive response. "Yes, I think that would be best. Not only would your father want me to look after you, but I think we need each other's help in running the plantation." He pulled the reins to stop the horses at the back door of the big house and came around to Penny's side of the wagon to help her down.

She gratefully took his hand and allowed him to escort her to the door.

"I'll pack my things and be back in the morning. Will you be all right tonight?"

Penny nodded.

He waited for a moment to see if she had

anything else to say.

She stood on her tiptoes and gave him a kiss on the cheek. "Thanks, Luke. I don't know what I'd do without you."

"Hopefully, you won't ever have to find out." He looked into her deep green eyes.

For a moment, she thought he was going to kiss her, but he quickly turned and walked through the puddles back to the wagon. He tipped his hat to her as he snapped the reins and rode off into the torrential storm.

As he drove off, she thought, *"That was silly of me. Why would Luke want to kiss me?"*

She climbed the stairs to the sounds of thunder and the flashes of lightning through the windows. It sounded like tonight's storm would be the worst they had seen in years, but she was too tired to care. She crawled into her bed and had a fitful night's sleep with dreams of her parents and of Luke. She was relieved to finally open her eyes to a sunny morning.

Luke arrived bright and early just as he had promised, and the two spent the morning in the office, going over the plantation's record books. They compared notes as they studied the books all afternoon and into the evening.

"This is too much. I don't know if I can do all this," she complained.

"Penny, don't worry, I know a lot about running the farm. I'll help in any way I can," he assured her. "We'll get through it together."

She pouted at him and he grinned back. She was grateful for his help and dependability. It was also nice to have her childhood friend back in her daily life.

As the days and weeks passed, she slowly but surely began to understand the business side of the plantation.

A month after her mother's funeral, Penny received some visitors from Liberty Baptist Church.

"Good morning, Miss Juzan," the men greeted her when she answered the door.

She recognized them immediately and smiled. "Good morning, gentlemen. What can I do for you today?"

The men, dressed in their best Sunday suits, told her they were having a fundraiser to raise money to repair the roof of the sanctuary. "A bad storm damaged it last month and it's going to cost more than we have in our coffers to replace it. So, we're holding an auction to raise money, and if you have anything to donate, we will gladly take it."

"Oh, my, I remember that storm. That was the evening we buried my mother."

"Yes, we heard about your loss and we're very sorry to lose Mrs. Juzan."

"Well, you know my mother loved the church, and if she were here, she would donate to your worthy cause. Let me look around and find some items for you. Would you come back in a few days and collect them?"

"We certainly will, Miss Juzan." And with that, they thanked her and were gone.

She followed the men outside and sat down on the steps to watch them leave. She allowed her thoughts to travel back to that stormy night. She missed her mother so much. Betty Juzan was a good woman. She also remembered riding back to the house with Luke in that storm. Luke Fisher was a good man. She felt safe and protected in his presence. He reminded her so much of her father. She wondered what her parents would think of her and Luke becoming a couple. She lifted her face to the sun, closed her eyes, and allowed the heat to surround her. After a few moments, she opened her eyes and shook her head. What was she thinking? Luke would never want a romantic relationship with her. They were like siblings. She stood up and went back in the house.

At supper that evening she told Luke about the church visitors. "So, I was wondering if you would help me search the attic for some items. Besides, you'd be a good person to carry anything we find down the stairs," she teased.

"You just want me around so I can lift heavy stuff?"

She laughed.

He nodded. "Sure, I'd be happy to help." He slurped a spoonful of soup. "Do you want to go up and look tomorrow?"

"Tomorrow would be perfect. I told the men to come back in a few days, and I'd like to be ready when they return." She offered him more bread, but he shook his head.

He leaned back in his chair and paused for a moment. "You know, digging through that old junk actually sounds like fun," he smiled.

His grin melted her heart. She hadn't seen him genuinely happy for such a long time. Perhaps tomorrow would begin the rekindling of the happiness that used to live in the house.

The following morning, they met in the hallway, both wearing old clothes. Penny wore her hair in a tight braid without a bonnet.

"I like your hair showing," Luke offered.

Penny smiled back at him, and they climbed the narrow staircase that led to the attic.

The large room was filled with dust and spider webs. "I guess it's been a long time since we've been up here," Penny commented as she wiped cobwebs from the air.

"I can't remember the last time I've been here. I guess it was that summer we had our make-believe store."

Penny giggled. "Oh my goodness. I'd forgotten about that."

They picked up one thing after the next, commenting about the last time they used or saw it. They had been looking around for quite a while when Penny ran across a stack of books.

"Luke, remember these?" She held one up. "We used to play with them when we were little...until Daddy took them all down to his office."

Luke walked over to her, picked up one of the books, and thumbed through it. "Yeah, we used to sell these in our pretend bookstore." He laughed.

Penny smiled at Luke. It was good to see her old friend happy. She looked down at the books and wrinkled her forehead.

He noticed her expression change and asked, "What are you thinking?"

"I seem to remember seeing my father sitting at his desk in his office writing in one of these. My mother must have brought them all back up here after his death." She thumbed across the spines, looking at the years written on them. She pulled out the most recent one marked 1841, opened it, and saw inventories and tables in the front, followed by long paragraphs that seemed to be a story, then a few blank pages. Then, she gasped.

"Yes, here it is."

Luke fell to his knees across from her and waited for her to tell him what it said.

"This is my father's handwriting." She pointed to the page.

The top of the page was dated "1901," and the script told of sending Carter Stuckey to retrieve the trunk from Lake Juzan. It described the long wait for a message from Carter. After the last entry in the journal, there was a piece of paper stuck between the pages. Penny pulled it out and looked at it. The outside read PIERRE JUZAN—URGENT. She recognized it as the wrinkled note she had delivered to her father the morning of his death. She unfolded it and read:

Great news, Mr. Juzan.

I have retrieved your long-lost trunk from Lake Juzan as you requested. I will be en route to you in Vicksburg as soon as this rain lets up. As it has been pouring the last two days, the roads are a muddy mess, so I'm sending you word of my success, and I will find an inn to stay at here in Lauderdale County until the roads are passable for the wagon.

Sincerely, Carter Stuckey

She stared at the paper and her jaw dropped. "Luke, do you remember Carter Stuckey?"

"Sure. White hair, beard, smoked a pipe. He was the overseer of the plantation for years."

"Whatever happened to him?"

Luke thought about it, then shrugged and shook his head. "I don't know. He just up and disappeared one day."

"This letter says he was in Lake Juzan retrieving a long-lost trunk. It says he recovered it and would be returning soon." She gently shook the paper toward Luke. "I remember handing my father this letter the day he died, but I don't remember seeing Carter Stuckey after my father's death."

"No, I don't, either. Your mother ran the farm after your father died. She ran it until the day I took over as the foreman."

* * *

Penny read the rest of the journal that night and learned of the missing gold. She immediately decided to find out what had happened to it, and within days, she was on her way to Lauderdale County, Mississippi. She learned that the sheriff back in 1901 was J.R. Temple. He had since retired and was living in a house on 8th Avenue in Meridian. She paid him a visit.

She knocked on the wooden frame of the screen door and the rattle reverberated across the screened porch. The kind face of a white-haired man with gray eyes greeted her warily.

"Yes, miss? May I help you?"

"Yes, sir. I'm looking for Sheriff Temple." Penny gave him her biggest and brightest smile.

He narrowed his eyes at her. "Well, that would be me, young lady, and who might you be?"

"Sheriff, my name is Penelope Juzan. I wonder if I might ask you a few questions."

"Questions about what?"

"I'm interested in a man who worked for my father in 1901. He sent my father a message that he was staying at an inn in town, and we never heard from him again. His name was Carter Stuckey."

The sheriff froze. He stared at her for a long time and didn't respond.

"Sheriff? Please, sir. I came all the way from Vicksburg to speak with you."

He sighed, turned away from the door, and walked into the house. "Oh, all right. Come on in." He didn't open the door for her and he didn't sound very enthusiastic.

She opened the creaking screen door and followed him into the cool darkness of the modest home. The place smelled musty. A worn and dirty flowered sofa sat in the living room to her left, along with a big chair that had seen better days long, long ago. She stood in the middle of the room and watched him light the wood-burning stove and place a black teakettle on top. He finally turned to her and gestured toward the small dining table to her right, then turned back to the stove. "Have a seat, Miss Juzan."

Penny pulled out a wooden chair that was covered with dust. She scanned the room to see if there were any feminine touches, as the house appeared to be owned by a bachelor. She saw nothing that would suggest a woman lived there. As the former sheriff stood at the wood-burning stove, she glanced at the back of his wrinkled shirt, hoping he wouldn't turn and see her wiping off the chair before she sat down. She held her handbag in her lap, as she wasn't sure if he would offer her some tea or kick her out in the next few minutes.

She was concerned when he began to cough violently. He pulled a cigarette off the shelf above the stove and lit it with a match. Penny remained silent and watched him exhale smoke between coughs. As his coughing spell subsided, the teakettle whistled. The sheriff used a pot holder to grab the hot kettle, and he poured two mugs of tea. He brought them to the table and placed one in front of Penny.

"Thank you," she said softly.

He turned back to the stove, snubbed out his cigarette on a plate, and then sat down at the table.

"Carter Stuckey, eh?"

Penny nodded and took a sip of her tea. It was extremely hot and just as weak.

Once the sheriff began telling her the story, he spoke for quite some time. She listened wordlessly, mesmerized by the tale. He told her the whole saga of the inn up on Chunky River and the innkeeper's victims. She sat with her mouth agape at the heinous story, and was even more stunned at the way it ended.

"The innkeeper's name was Stuckey—Thomas Stuckey."

"Stuckey?"

"Yes, it appears he took the name of one of his victims.

"So, Carter Stuckey was one of the victims?"

"Yes, ma'am. Carter Stuckey had something in his pocket with his name on it when we uncovered his body, so we know for sure he was murdered at the inn. No one ever came looking for him, and we didn't know who to contact about his death, so we moved his remains to Concord Cemetery and buried him in an unmarked grave."

"Well, no one knew he was here except my father. My father died about the same time and I just recently found his journals, which led me here."

The two sat in silence for a few minutes while

Penny absorbed the gravity of the tale.

"Miss Juzan, why are you looking for Carter Stuckey now, a decade later?"

"Oh, um, well, he had something of my father's, something of great importance. I'm afraid I didn't know about it until a few weeks ago when I found my father's journals."

"And what was this item of great importance?" He wrinkled his brow at her.

"It was a trunk, sir."

"A trunk?" The sheriff ran his fingers down his stubble and shook his head. "I don't remember finding any trunk at the inn, but I'll tell you who might know. The only survivor of the whole incident was a young boy. He was maybe twelve or thirteen years old at the time. He was a blond, blue-eyed boy named Levi Stuckey. The moment his father—the murderer—was hung, the boy disappeared. I searched for him for years but he'd simply vanished. If he's still alive somewhere, he'd be about twenty-two now. Maybe he knows something about your missing trunk. Maybe he has it himself."

She nodded. "Maybe he does."

"I don't know that you'll have any luck finding him, though. I sure didn't. You should also take a ride out to the old inn and speak with the new owners of the property. Of course, it's just a private home now, not an inn anymore, but you could check with them and see if they ever ran across your trunk."

"Thank you, sheriff. I'll do just that."

She thanked him for the information and bid him a good day. He wished her luck in her search as the screen door slammed behind her. She turned and waved but he was already back inside the house.

She hopped on her wagon and traveled down to the old inn. The owners said nothing of value had been found on the property when they bought it at auction. There was nothing except old furniture, household items, and a horse corral that looked like it had been built from bits and pieces of other things. The man spoke about that corral for a long time, and Penny could hardly escape.

Penny spent the night at the Hotel Meridian near Union Station, tossing and turning in the uncomfortable bed as she went over every word of the tale the sheriff had told her. She stayed up most of the night giving the situation much thought, and by dawn, she came to the conclusion the only place the trunk could possibly be was in the possession of Levi Stuckey. She also deduced if he had that much gold, he wouldn't be living in a shack in the back hills of Mississippi. He'd be hobnobbing with the rich. She returned to Vicksburg and sold the plantation to finance her venture into the world of the elite. Luke was quite upset about her decision, but she would not be deterred. She would find this Levi Stuckey, and she would get her family's gold back. She would make sure her father's death had not been in vain. How hard could it be to find a rich twenty-two-year old, blond, blue-eyed millionaire named Levi Stuckey?

Part IV: Unrequited Love

"Penny spent the next few months traveling through wealthy circles, searching for Levi Stuckey. She finally found him in Georgia at a place where the rich and famous gathered—a place called Jekyll Island. He had changed his name from Levi Stuckey to Levi Temple, which Penny found most amusing. He had taken the sheriff's name, but he wasn't an upstanding, law-abiding citizen like his eponym. Levi was a cold-blooded killer. He murdered at least four people she knew of while she was on the island. He killed them either to get his own way or to keep them quiet about his secrets."

"What happened to him?" asked the younger boy.

"And did Penny find the gold?" asked the older one.

His chair creaked as he rocked. He looked out at the menacing storm clouds, debating which question to answer first. The sky had darkened to black and green with the coming storm and the Mississippi sunset had been replaced by a dusky gloom. He looked at the boys.

"Levi was eventually found out and taken into custody by the local Georgia sheriff. The last time Penny saw him, he was in the back of the sheriff's wagon, on his way to be tried and most

likely hung for his crimes."

"What about the gold?" the older boy asked again.

He nodded. "Yes, Penny did find the gold. After seventy years and four generations, the gold was finally in the hands of the Juzan family."

"What about the curse?" the younger boy asked.

"Well, the curse certainly wasn't finished yet, and the future held even more surprises for Penny."

Chapter 25

After finding the trunk of gold on Jekyll Island, Penny and Luke rendezvoused in Birmingham and boarded a train bound for Vicksburg. Armed with a vast amount of wealth, they tried to buy their plantation back. Sadly, the man who'd bought it from Penny refused to sell it back for any amount of money. He said not only was it a prosperous property, but his wife had fallen in love with the antebellum plantation home and would never forgive him if he sold it out from under her.

Sad and homeless, Penny and Luke sat in a diner on the banks of the Mississippi, sipped coffee, and pondered what their next move should be.

"Well, what should we do now?" Luke asked after he had ordered a slice of sweet potato pie.

"I'm not sure," replied Penny. "We have plenty of money to do anything we want... anything except buy back our plantation, apparently." She pouted as she poured some cream into her coffee.

Luke stirred his coffee and placed the spoon

down on the edge of the saucer. "Where would you *like* to live?"

"I'd *like* to live here, but I don't want to live in a different house. I don't want to live here unless we live in our house," she pouted.

"That's not going to happen, Penny." He took a sip of his coffee, watching her over the brim of the cup.

"I know." She removed her wide-brimmed hat, placed it on the seat beside her, and smoothed back her hair with her palm. "I don't want to head north and live around those rich Yankees, that's for sure." She gazed out the window at the boats passing by on the river. "I've always love the water. What about moving to Lake Juzan?"

"Why would you want to go there?"

"Why not? It's our family's property—our heritage. How about we go there and open a new inn and a tavern?"

"Have you ever been there?"

"No, but what I saw of Lauderdale County when I went to visit the sheriff was beautiful, so I imagine it's very nice. Maybe we could make it as lovely as Jekyll Island, you know, a place where the rich come to spend their money."

"Would you really want to cater to those people like you were their maid?"

The waitress plopped the plate of sweet potato pie in front of Luke and asked if she could get them anything else. They both shook their heads.

Luke sliced his fork into the pie, shoved a bite into his mouth, and continued speaking with his mouth full. "And those people would never accept me. I'd end up washing their dishes."

"You're right about them, but we could still

open a small inn for travelers. They'd be grateful to have nice lodgings to stay in when they travel through the county."

"Yes, I guess we could do that." He sipped his coffee. "What about your grandma Marguerite?"

"What about her?"

"She gave up everything to get her family away from that place, and now you're going to waltz back there on purpose?"

"Well, Luke, according to *you*, she gave up everything to get her family away from a curse created by *your* great-grandmother. A curse that obviously doesn't exist. We have the gold now and nothing has happened to us. I think Grandma Marguerite was simply a superstitious woman."

Luke thought about that for a while as he finished eating his pie. He hoped Penny was right, but after so many had died in the quest for the gold, he wasn't so sure. She was correct about one thing, though—nothing had happened to them so far. Maybe this was finally his opportunity to make a new life with Penny. He had admitted to her while they were on Jekyll Island that he was in love with her. He didn't realize just how much he cared for her until she had gone to look for Levi, and he was miserable without her. When he first saw her and Levi together, he felt such jealousy in his gut, he thought he'd explode. He loved this woman. He had always loved her. When he told her so in the island, she didn't reciprocate, but that was all right. He knew he had shocked her with his proclamation of love, and he knew deep in her heart she loved him, too. He saw it in her green eyes the night they buried her mother. He almost kissed her that night, but he didn't want to play into her vulnerability after just losing her mother. Hopefully, this was a new beginning for them and she would soon realize how much she loved him. Hopefully, they'd soon be happy together as a couple. But truthfully, even if she never loved him back, he didn't want to live without her. He needed to be with her. She was like air to him. He couldn't survive without her. Wherever Penelope Juzan wanted to go, he would go, too.

He grinned. "Lake Juzan it is, then."

Chapter 26

Luke and Penny hired eight workers to build their new inn on the shore of Lake Juzan. The frame went up quickly. The upper floor consisted of six bedrooms and the lower floor contained two bedrooms for Penny and Luke, along with a parlor for guests to gather. The front door entered right into the parlor and the back of the room connected to a hallway that led to the back door. Luke had already laid the stone path from the back door to the tavern. The tavern, which would be completed next, would house the dining room and the kitchen. They planned to build a half dozen tables and a bar that ran the length of the room, along with stools to nest under the bar. They figured they could fit thirty people in the room for supper. They'd probably never have near that many guests, but better to have too much room than not enough.

Penny planted fruit trees on the left side of the stone path, and together she and Luke built a chicken coop on the right side. They surrounded the small yard with a picket fence to keep the chickens enclosed, and they broke ground for a garden behind the inn, in the place a small cottage once stood. They had to tear the small building down to make room for the garden. They used the stones from it to lay out the foundation for a smokehouse that Luke planned to finish someday.

The new inn stood in the exact spot where the original inn had stood. They knew so because they had to clear the remnants of the old building. It had decayed and fallen down since it was abandoned over fifty years ago. Penny hoped the new building would last much longer. Following her demanding schedule for completion, it would take the rest of the summer for the workers to finish the buildings, so for now, Penny, Luke, and the builders all slept in tents.

After a couple weeks of intense construction, Penny found it difficult to keep up the pace she had dictated. She was so very tired. Even Luke had mentioned on occasion that she looked pale, demanding that she sit and rest. She never told him about throwing up her breakfast for the last two months, and she certainly never told him she had missed her last three periods.

The last time he demanded she rest, she sat under the shade of a pecan tree and watched the workers pounding nails into the inn's new roof. She absentmindedly rubbed her hands across her protruding belly. There was no doubt about it—she was pregnant. She wouldn't be able to hide it much longer. What bothered her more than a pregnancy out of wedlock was the fact she had been with only one man. The father was none other than Levi Stuckey and the child was conceived on Jekyll Island. She didn't know how to break the news to Luke, but she knew she would have to do so very soon.

That evening they ate supper at the table next to the tents. After he gobbled two slices of bread and butter, she watched him dig his fork into some green beans and shovel them into his mouth.

He stopped eating and looked at her green eyes in the dim light of the lantern between them. "What are you looking at and why aren't you eating?"

"I don't have much of an appetite, I guess, and there's something I need to tell you, but I'm not sure how you're going to take it. I'm deciding whether I should let you finish eating first."

He pushed his plate away and wiped his mouth on his shirtsleeve. "I'm done eating. What do you want to tell me?"

"There's no easy way to say this, Luke, so..." She closed her eyes and took a deep breath and held it, trying to build some courage to say the words out loud. Then she blurted out, "I'm pregnant."

He stared at her blankly.

She opened her eyes and looked at him. As she awaited a response, she noticed he wasn't breathing either. He didn't move. The silence between them was so uncomfortable, she finally asked, "Well? Don't you have anything to say?"

"It's his, isn't it?" His temples pulsed and he clenched his teeth.

She nodded.

His eyes darkened. He was so sad, and she didn't know how to stop him from hurting. Maybe she did feel more for him than she had admitted to. His heart was breaking right in front of her and hers began to shatter as well. They looked at each other for a long time.

Finally he spoke. "It's not proper to have a child while you're unwed. What if we get married and tell everyone the child is mine?"

"Luke, it's probably going to have blond hair and blue eyes. No one would ever believe it's yours." She paused before she delivered the final blow. "And I don't want to get married."

He propped his elbows on the table and rested his chin against his tented fingers. "So, what do you want to do, Penny?" The question came out terser than he meant for it to.

She shrugged. "Nothing much I can do, I guess."

His eyes were deep black pools filled with pain, and her heart overflowed with tenderness for him. She wished she could take it all back, but it was too late.

"I just wanted you to know," she said softly.

He swallowed hard. "Thank you for telling me."

She reached across the table to touch his hand, but he pulled away from her. He rose and left the table without a word. She watched his silhouette in the dimming light as he walked away, heading down to the lake.

Chapter 27

On a crisp October morning, Penny delivered a healthy, blond-haired, blue-eyed, eight-pound baby boy. She named him Theo after her father, even though she wasn't sure her father would have approved of her giving birth to a child out of wedlock. She mentioned that fact to Luke, and he reminded her Theodore Juzan couldn't have been more supportive when Luke's mother had him out of wedlock. Penny had never given much thought to that situation. Luke always had Theodore as a father, but never had his own. Penny never questioned it; it was just the way it had always been. She realized Luke was right. Her father was a good man, a kind man. He loved Luke like he was his own son. He would have acknowledged her predicament and accepted her child with open arms. He would have loved baby Theo.

Over the next few months, Penny, Luke, and Theo quickly became a tight-knit family, with Luke looking after the boy almost as much as Penny did. As Penny had predicted, no one believed Theo was Luke's child. People in town gave Luke strange looks when they carted the babe to the general store or the stables. Luke ignored them. He loved the boy and no one could ever take that fact away. It didn't matter to Penny or Luke if strangers understood their family or not.

As summer settled its warm blanket on Lake Juzan, Luke took eight-month-old Theo into town to pick up some supplies for the inn. They had been extremely busy since the inn opened with every room filled every night, and on this particular morning, Penny busied herself with cleaning rooms from last night's guests. She had prepared the mop water and was just about to begin cleaning the parlor floor when heard a sharp knock on the front door. She wondered if Luke had forgotten something, for it was highly unusual for travelers to stop by the inn so early in the day. She figured he was probably holding little Theo in his arms and couldn't open the door himself. She wiped her hands on her apron, smoothed her hair back from her face, and opened the door.

The person standing on the other side made her gasp. It wasn't Luke. It wasn't a customer. It was Levi Stuckey. His blond hair alit with the rising sun behind him.

"I can't believe I finally found you." He beamed and reached out for her.

She quickly took a step backward to avoid the contact.

"Why are you here?" she demanded.

"I've been searching for you for months and months. I remembered you told me you lived in Vicksburg, so I went there but you weren't there. The next place I thought I should try was your family's lake, so I traveled to Lake Juzan, and here you are. I'm so glad you're here!" The grin on his face was sincere.

"I thought you were in jail...or dead."

He rolled his eyes and chuckled. "Those outhouses they call jails are a joke. I spent one night there, watched the ignorant jail keeper forget to lock the door when he served me breakfast, and I walked out in broad daylight. I've been traveling, searching for you, ever since."

She pushed on the door, attempting to slam it in his face, but he was faster and stuck his boot in the doorway. He lowered his voice. "Penny, listen to me. I'm not here for revenge, and I don't want the gold back."

She peeked around the door at his face. His expression looked genuine, but she felt a trickle of sweat drip down her back as her heart pounded wildly. "Then why *are* you here, Levi?"

He forced the door open a couple of inches and she was powerless to stop him. "I'm here for you. I've never met a woman like you, and I'm in love with you, Penelope Juzan. I want to build a life with you, a normal life of a man and woman in love."

"In love?" Even though he said he wasn't there to harm her, she still felt her fear and adrenaline rise. Her ears felt hot. Her breathing wouldn't slow down. She felt like a caged animal about to go to slaughter. This man was crazy.

He smiled sweetly. "Yeah, in love. I want to get married and raise a family and be happy."

"A family?" The thought of Theo popped into her head and she knew her face had gone pale.

"Yes, lots and lots of children." He laughed. "Wouldn't that be great?"

She glanced over his shoulder at the road, praying Luke and Theo wouldn't return from town until she could get rid of Levi. Levi would know with one glance that Theo was his.

"Levi, listen, I don't understand why you think you love me. You don't even know me." She held the door firmly.

"I know all I need to know. I know every time I look into your beautiful eyes, my heart quickens. I know in the beginning we had a great time on Jekyll Island. I know I want to have more times like that with you. Please, give us a chance, Penny."

She furrowed her brow and shook her head. "There is no *us,* Levi."

"There can be. Tell me you want that just as much as I do."

Her face remained stern. "No, Levi, I don't. I don't want to be with you. I don't love you, and if you don't leave immediately, I'll tell the sheriff where to find you."

Levi's face, previously filled with affection and desire, turned dangerously solemn as his eyes transformed from blue to storm-cloud gray. His jaw twitched as her stared at her.

"It's him, isn't it?"

"Who?"

"The Indian?"

"What? No! It's just I don't want anything to do with you. You're a murderer, and now you're a fugitive. What kind of life could anyone have with you?"

"This isn't you speaking, Penny. I know it's him. You're seeing that Indian behind my back, aren't you?"

"No, I'm not. I'm not seeing anyone, and even

if I was, it wouldn't be behind your back, because we're not together."

Levi's expression softened as he relaxed and leaned against the doorjamb. "Did I ever tell you what happened to my mother?"

"What? No."

"My father caught her sneaking around behind his back. She was carrying on with an Indian."

"What? Why are you telling me this?"

"So you'll know the consequences."

"What consequences?" She already knew Levi's brand of consequences. She had seen them many times on the island as girls were found dead. A shiver went up her spine and she felt her knees go weak. She struggled to remain standing.

"My father killed them both—my mother and her Indian lover. He strangled them."

Penny backed away from the door. That's how Levi had killed those people on Jekyll Island. He strangled them. He was insane. She had to get away from him.

He pushed the door all the way open, and it slammed against the wall, rattling the windows. He stepped into the room. Penny turned to run but he grabbed for her. Fortunately, the only thing he got his hand on was the cleaning rag she had tucked into her apron. Missing his target only made him angrier.

"Penny!" he yelled loudly. "Don't make me come after you."

He stomped toward her, but she had already ran down the hall and reached the back door. She yanked it open and fled into the backyard. She ran down the stone path and the chickens squawked as she ripped open the side gate and ran in the only direction she knew she could hide. She headed down to the lake.

Levi was close behind. Very close.

Chapter 28

A few hours later, Luke returned from his trip to town with a wagon full of supplies and a sleeping infant. Theo didn't wake as Luke gently lifted him from the wagon and carried him into the inn. Luke paused for a moment at the front door as he found it strange that the door was wide open. When he entered, he noticed the mop and pail of water sitting idle in the middle of the room. He didn't call out for Penny as he didn't want to wake Theo. He placed the babe in his crib in Penny's room and quietly closed the door behind him.

"Penny?" he called quietly as he returned to the parlor. She didn't answer. He went upstairs to see if she was cleaning. "Penny?" He checked each room, but she wasn't anywhere to be found, and the untidy guest rooms looked exactly as they did when he had left earlier that morning. He figured she must be in the tavern, so he headed down the stairs toward the back door. He stopped and checked the temperature of the mop water in the pail. Penny always mopped with hot water because she said it cleaned better. The water in the pail was tepid and the floor hadn't been mopped because there were muddy boot prints leading from the front door to the back door. He frowned as he looked at the odd prints. "Why would she go to all that trouble to prepare the mop water then not mop the floor?"

He walked toward the back door and found it too was open. He stepped out onto the path and noticed the gate was also ajar and the chickens were out in the yard. Penny never let the chickens out of their enclosure. She said if anyone was going to eat their chickens, it would be them, not the coyotes. Something was amiss. Why was the gate left open and where was Penny?

He walked down the stone path and entered the tavern. In the light of the open doorway, he saw dirty dishes crowding the tables. "Penny?" No answer. He entered the kitchen and through the light of the window he saw dirty pots and pans resting in the sink and on the wood-burning stove. He bent down and looked at the bottom of the stove. Ashes were still piled high from yesterday's fire. He returned to the dining room and lit one of the lanterns. "Penny?" Nothing had been touched. Everything was exactly where it had been last night.

"Penny?!" he yelled louder, but there was no answer. "Where could she be?"

Maybe she's down at the boat dock. He hurried down the trail toward the lake, hoping over twigs and stumps as he ran, and as he grew closer, his hands began to sweat with a strange foreboding. They had been happy and without incident for a year and a half, but as the lake came into view, the curse weighed heavily on his mind. *What if something happened? Where is she? Where could she have disappeared to?*

He emerged from the woods into the clearing. The sun glistened on the water like shimmering diamonds. Nothing looked disturbed around the dock. Their rowboat, used strictly by the guests, was tied securely to the dock. Fishing poles leaned against the tree closest to the water. He looked across the lake and saw nothing unusual. "Penny!" he yelled. No answer came except the cawing of a crow on the far shore. He didn't think he should leave Theo alone for very long to go look for Penny, but the baby was asleep, and he needed to find her. He set out to circle the lake and prayed it would be a useless journey. He hoped he would return to find her mopping the parlor and chastising him for leaving Theo alone.

A half hour into his trek, he arrived at the far side of the lake, and noticed the red mud on the shore was filled with boot prints. As far as he knew, no guest had ever walked out this far. There were so many prints, it looked as if there had been a scuffle. He knelt down and examined the prints. There were two distinct sets—a man's boot and a smaller woman's shoe. Suddenly his heart felt as if it had stopped. He couldn't catch his breath when he realized the man's print looked the same as the muddy print on the floor at the inn. Still on bended knee, he called Penny's name over and over as he scanned the shore. It was then he saw the corner of her white apron gently billowing in the tall grasses to his left. He had passed right by that spot only moments ago, but hadn't seen anything from that vantage point.

He ran to the apron and there in the tall reeds of the marsh was his beautiful Penny, her eyes glassy and unblinking. He stepped into the ankle-deep swampy water and knelt down next to her. He shook her by the shoulders, repeating her name over and over. She didn't respond. She was dead.

He hugged her tightly in his arms for a long time before he held her afar to look at her face. He gasped when he noticed it, and he softly ran his finger across the markings on her neck. There was a dark bruising around her neck that contrasted against her pale white skin. He shook his head in disbelief. He knew exactly what had happened. He didn't know how it was possible, but he knew who did this.

He sobbed as he lifted Penny's lifeless body and carried her back to the inn.

Chapter 29

Luke took Theo down the road to a neighbor's house and asked the sweet lady to watch the babe for a day or so, to which she kindly obliged. He then returned to the inn to take care of Penny's remains. He lovingly and tearfully sponged the red mud from her face and hair, whispering over and over to her how much he loved her. He then dressed her in her dark purple velvet gown. She had bought a few expensive gowns when she went to Jekyll Island, but she never wore any of them since returning to Mississippi. The dresses remained in the wardrobe, gathering dust. He remembered the first time he saw her in this purple gown. He had gone to Jekyll Island to find her and tell her that he loved her. He stood in the second floor window and watched her stroll across the lawn in the evening light. She floated like an angel. She looked like a princess. She looked so incredibly stunning in the twilight, and he was overjoyed to see her after long months of missing her.

After he dressed her, he gently combed and

braided her hair, then he cradled her in his arms and carried her down to the dock. He gently placed her in the rowboat and rowed out to the middle of the lake. Tears streamed down his cheeks as he lifted her petite body, kissed her softly on the lips, and rolled her over the side. A small splash sounded as she entered the water and ripples steadily spread across the entire lake. He watched her gown turn dark as it soaked up water, and slowly she sank. The last thing to disappear below the surface was her long braid which glowed in the evening sun. Then she was gone.

He watched the ripples move across the lake until they gradually disappeared. He was looking toward the red sunset when a movement in the direction of the inn caught his eye. A man was standing in the shadows under a tree. He knew exactly who it was.

He turned the boat around and rowed back to shore.

Chapter 30

As twilight enveloped the lake, Luke tied up the boat and walked to where he had seen the man. He knew what the man's boot prints looked like so he didn't have any trouble tracking him. The man seemed to be walking aimlessly, mostly in circles. Finally under the cloak of near darkness, he followed the boot prints back to the inn.

Luke quietly circled the building and found all the doors closed. He tiptoed around to each window and peered in. The parlor was dark. He peeked into his bedroom window; it was also dark. He neared Penny's bedroom window and saw a dim light radiating from the window. A shadow crossed the window as someone walked between it and a lantern. He crouched down and peeked into the window, and when he looked over the windowsill, he saw him.

Levi Stuckey was standing in the corner of the room, gazing into Theo's crib. Luke froze, feeling flames of adrenalin rise up the back of his neck. He couldn't seem to catch his next breath. Until this very moment, it had never dawned on him that if Levi saw the boy, he would instantly recognize him as his own son. Until this moment, it had never occurred to him that Levi Stuckey was even alive. That murderer should have been hung a long time ago. The possibility of Levi getting anywhere near Theo made Luke's heart beat wildly. He clenched his fists. That would happen over Luke's dead body. He raised Theo, and Theo was his son, not Levi's.

Luke pulled his pearl-handled Colt from his waistband and entered the inn through the back door. He marched straight toward Penny's room without even trying to silence his footsteps. He pushed open the door which bounced against the wall, and he stood stone still in the doorway. Levi was still staring into the crib and didn't turn to face Luke.

"What are you doing here?" Luke growled.

Levi continued to stare at the crib. "Whose crib is this?"

"That's none of your business. Why aren't you in jail?"

Levi turned toward Luke and saw the gun. "So, you *are* here. I knew she was messing around with you." Levi thumbed over his shoulder at the crib. "I suppose there's an Indian child who sleeps in this bed."

Luke hesitated, wondering if telling Levi the truth would hurt him more than allowing him to believe otherwise. He wanted to do nothing more than to hurt this man.

His hesitation was the wrong thing to do. Levi's eyes grew large.

"When did Penny have a baby?"

Without thinking, Luke answered, "He was born in October."

The men stared at each other for a moment.

Levi then looked down at the floor with his brow furrowed, obviously calculating the months that had passed. He slowly looked back at Luke. "I have a son?" he finally asked.

Luke didn't answer, but he felt bile rise in his throat and thought for a moment he might throw up.

"Why didn't she tell me?"

"Would it have changed anything? You would have killed her anyway."

Levi's forehead wrinkled as he looked at the crib and shook his head. "Maybe not," he mumbled.

Luke had had enough of the questions. "Why did you kill her?" Tears filled Luke's eyes and he raised the gun to Levi's head and cocked the hammer.

Levi didn't flinch. Softly he repeated, "Why didn't she tell me?" Then he looked at Luke with tears in his eyes. "I loved her, you know."

Luke's jaw twitched in hatred. "You don't kill people you love."

Luke squeezed the trigger.

Part V: The Gold

He sighed heavily as the two boys gawked at him. After a very long pause, he continued. "So, I abandoned the inn and I brought your daddy back here to Vicksburg. I raised him all by myself, as if he were my own. I've loved him every moment of his life, and I knew I had to protect him and get him away from that lake and that curse."

"But Grandpa Luke, if you have all that gold, why do you live in this rundown shack?" *asked the older boy, the winds whipping wildly in his hair.*

"Yeah, why don't you live in a big castle or something?" *asked the younger one.*

"There's no gold anymore, boys. The very next day, I rowed that cursed trunk out to the middle of the lake, and I tossed it over the side of the boat. As far as I know, it's still buried in the black, swampy waters of Lake Juzan—and that's where it needs to stay."

He gestured for the boys to come to him, and he gave them a long hug and patted them on their heads. "You boys run along now and get home before it rains."

"Thank you for the story, Grandpa Luke," *they*

chorused.

He watched them jump off the porch and scurry across the field toward their house. They were good boys. He knew they'd never go after the gold. At least he hoped his story was frightening enough, they'd never want to tempt the curse. The gold needed to remain in the bottom of the lake. It wasn't just a scary tale. It was real. The gold was real. The curse was real. He had seen both with his own eyes.

Thunder boomed loudly in the sky and the first fat drops of rain began to fall. He remained in his rocking chair, slowly rocking back and forth, watching the black clouds draw closer.

THE END

Author's Notes

The legends of Stuckey's Bridge and Lake Juzan are very similar stories. They are both said to have occurred in the same area in Mississippi, both contain details of an innkeeper killing for riches, and both locations are said to be haunted to this day by the perpetrators and the victims. Through "The Legend of Stuckey's Bridge," "Stuckey's Legacy," and "Stuckey's Gold," I weaved and twisted the tales together, not in an effort to condense them into one story, but perhaps in an effort to see both sides of the same gold coin. Some of the names and locations in this book are factual, some are part of the legends, and some are only in my imagination.

Many thanks go out to those who provided support as this story was written:

Elyse Dinh-McCrillis—www.theeditninja.com

Jen Quist—www.jenqphotography.com

Rob Hess—book designer

my dear family and friends in and around Lauderdale County, Mississippi

and my friends and colleagues at sea: Matthew Tobin and Conrad Askland.

About the Author

Lori Crane is a member of the United Daughters of the Confederacy, Daughters of the American Revolution, United States Daughters of 1812, and the Screen Actors Guild-American Federation of Television and Radio Artists

She is a native Mississippi belle currently residing in greater Nashville, Tennessee. She's a professional musician by night and an indie author by day.

Books by Lori Crane

Okatibbee Creek Series
Okatibbee Creek
An Orphan's Heart
Elly Hays

Stuckey's Bridge Trilogy
The Legend of Stuckey's Bridge
Stuckey's Legacy: The Legend Continues
Stuckey's Gold: The Curse of Lake Juzan

Culpepper Saga
I, John Culpepper
John Culpepper the Merchant
John Culpepper, Esquire
Culpepper's Rebellion

Other Titles
Savannah's Bluebird
Witch Dance
The Culpepper-Fairfax Scandal
On This Day: A Perpetual Calendar for Family Genealogy

For more information, please visit
www.LoriCrane.com
or email LoriCraneAuthor@gmail.com

The following is an excerpt from

THE LEGEND OF
STUCKEY'S BRIDGE

the first in the Stuckey's Bridge Trilogy

1942, Lauderdale County, Mississippi

Billy yanked up on his fishing pole. His eight-year-old brother asked, "Did you catch somethin'?"

Billy frowned as he watched the tip of his pole arc. The line grew taut. "Naw, I think I'm just snagged," he grumbled.

"Oh, I though you got a catfish."

"I wish. I think I'm stuck on somethin'." He lifted his pole again, reeling in an inch or two of the line.

"Maybe you caught one of Old Man Stuckey's boots."

"Don't even say that, Bobby. It gives me the creeps."

The warm afternoon sun quickly disappeared behind ominous dark clouds, leaving the boys in an eerie dusk one usually witnesses just before nightfall.

Bobby looked up. "It's gonna rain. You better get that line in so we can go."

Billy looked up, too. A gust of wind caught the

front wisp of his brown hair and gave him a chill.

"You know, everyone says he's still here," Bobby snickered.

"Who?"

"Old Man Stuckey."

"Yeah, I know, but I'd rather not think about it. Besides, I'm a little busy at the moment." Billy wrinkled his forehead as he tugged on the line again, ever so slowly bringing it closer.

Bobby yelled into the air. "Old Man Stuckey, jump in there and unsnag that line." He giggled.

Billy didn't think it was funny and gave his younger brother a nasty look. "Don't call him," he whispered as if someone might hear him, even though he knew there wasn't a soul within miles of them.

Bobby rose from his seat on the bank, leaving his line dangling in the murky water. "Here, let me help you." He walked in front of Billy and reached out over the river, trying to grab the clear fishing line.

Billy lifted the pole into the air a third time, bending the tip. "Whatever it is, it's coming. It's just slow."

"Maybe it's the noose they hung him with." Bobby laughed.

Billy didn't.

The sunny afternoon was transforming into an oncoming storm, and the clouds were rolling in fast— gloomy, thick, menacing clouds. The breeze rustled Billy's hair again, making him shiver.

To the right of the young boys stood Stuckey's Bridge—a ninety-year-old bridge, one hundred twelve feet long, with a plank bottom and iron framework across the top. Some people fished from the top of the bridge, but Billy refused to step onto it. Bobby teased him incessantly about his fear of Old Man Stuckey's ghost, but Billy accepted the teasing and stayed firmly on the bank. The only reason he came out here at all was to catch the *big* catfish, and *they* lived under the bridge. As far as he knew, across the river stood nothing but trees and brush and the occasional woodland animal. In his twelve years of life, he never dared go across the bridge to see if there was more.

Bobby grabbed the line and took a step back, pulling it as he moved. "What the heck you got on here?"

When Bobby let go, Billy spun the reel, bringing in the line a foot or so. "I don't know, probably just a branch or some leaves from the bottom."

"Well, whatever it is, it's heavy." Bobby stepped forward to get another handful of the line.

A crow flew overhead, barely maintaining its airborne status in the strong gusts of wind. Billy looked up for a moment, thinking the crow to be a bad omen. His hands began to sweat on the cork handle of his fishing pole. He decided at that very moment it was time to go, and they both needed to bring their lines in quickly. "Bobby, I got it from here. You should pull in your line so we can get home. Looks like a big storm comin'."

Bobby looked up at the sky. "Yeah, okay." He let go of Billy's line and walked back over to his fishing spot. A quick movement on the other side of the river caught his eye. "What was that?"

"What was what?" said Billy, still concentrating on his line.

"Over there." Bobby pointed to the left across the river. "I saw somethin' in the trees."

Billy looked over but didn't see anything. "Probably a possum or somethin'." Then Billy heard something in the brush. He froze.

Bobby heard it, too. "I told you I saw somethin'. Maybe a bobcat?"

Thunder cracked like a cannon above the boys' heads and made them jump. Bobby grabbed his pole and frantically reeled his line in. It was quickly growing dark and the wind was increasingly stronger. He watched Billy pull and tug at the line.

"It's almost free," Billy assured him. "It's comin' faster."

Bobby looked at the other side of the river. "Dang! There it is again. There's somethin' over there all right."

Billy glanced across the river, but with the dimming light, he couldn't see anything even if it was there. He pulled his line harder. A twig snapped across the river. Both boys darted their gazes in that direction but saw nothing but darkening woods.

"Maybe it's him!" Bobby teased.

"Stop it! Don't be stupid, Bobby."

Billy slowly but deliberately reeled in the line. He pointed the tip of his pole toward the water to keep it from snapping with the weight of the mystery catch, and he kept turning the reel. A drop of rain fell on his forehead, mingled with the nervous sweat on his brow, and gave him another shiver.

"Hurry up, Billy. We're gonna get soaked."

"I am hurrying. I don't want to break my line."

The crow sounded loudly from across the river, and shot straight up above the tree line as fast as an arrow released from a bow. The boys looked that way, knowing something was in the woods, just out of sight.

Another branch snapped.

"What the heck is that?" Bobby sounded nervous, staring into the encroaching darkness on the other side of the river.

Billy didn't answer. He was absorbed in the blob he was dragging across the top of the murky water.

Bobby looked out at the greenish-brown blob. "You got nothin' but leaves. Let's go."

Billy pulled the blob onto the edge of the bank and laid his pole on the ground. He moved toward the blob to dislodge his hook, and noticed something shining in the blob. *What is that? It's shimmering. What the...?*

Another branch snapped across the river.

"Come on, Billy. We gotta go. Now."

"Hold on," Billy said as he grabbed a stick and poked into the blob, separating the leaves and muck.

Yes, there was something shiny. *Something gold.*

Thunder rumbled. A rustling sound came from across the river, making Bobby look in that direction again. Heavy, fat raindrops splattered on their heads, and dead leaves began to whirl around the banks of the river in the increasing winds. *It's something round.* The crow cawed noisily. Another twig snapped. *It's a watch.* Thunder roared again. *On a gold chain.* Lightning lit the sky in a jagged pulse for a few short seconds. The wind intensified.

"What is that?" Bobby asked.

"It's a pocket watch." Billy reached down and rubbed the mud off the front of the watch. He cocked his head to the side and saw a single T embossed in the gold. Simultaneously, the thunder roared, the crow cawed, the rustle across the river grew louder, and to their right, a giant splash scared both boys into standing straight up.

They stared, mouths agape, in the direction of the bridge. Right under it, the water rippled in a circle as if something very, very large had just been dropped off the bridge. Thunder rumbled again. The water rippled more. The boys froze. An inch above the water in the center of the ripple was an eerie green glow. Instead of dissipating as they expanded, the ripples seemed to grow larger and higher in the ever-growing circle, as if the ocean tide was causing waves to come ashore.

The boys didn't look at each other. They didn't communicate. They turned at the same time and ran away as fast as their feet would carry them. They didn't grab their fishing poles. They didn't look back.

Lightning flashed while raindrops splattered the rocks, turning them from gray to brown. As the storm strengthened, the ripples inched up onto the bank, and little by little, pulled the gold pocket watch back into the murky depths.

The following is an excerpt from

STUCKEY'S LEGACY:
THE LEGEND CONTINUES

the second in the Stuckey's Bridge Trilogy

December 31, 1911 11:59 p.m.

"...five...four...three...two...one...Happy New Year!" the crowd chanted in unison and the orchestra began to play "Auld Lang Syne." Balloons fell from the ceiling and confetti was tossed from the mezzanine. It fluttered to the floor, covering couples who clung together on the ballroom's massive dance floor. Wine flowed and lovers kissed, and twenty-two-year-old Levi stood off to the side, sipping his champagne, observing the festivities with a mixture of apathy and loathing.

A gentleman in a crumpled tuxedo, heading toward the bar, staggered by him and nodded. Levi coldly nodded back, hoping the intoxicated man wouldn't stop to chat. He was here to observe and mingle, not to spend the evening listening to a slurring drunkard. It had taken him a decade to get into this elite circle and he wasn't going to let some sot spoil it. He downed the remaining liquid, plopped his empty champagne glass on the nearest table, and quickly moved across the room.

Following a magnificent dinner of pheasant and turkey in the Grand Dining Room, he had thus far spent the evening strolling around the luxurious Jekyll Island Club, chatting with people with familiar surnames—Firestone, Carnegie, Rockefeller, Vanderbilt. He introduced himself to them as Levi Temple, a business partner of the late Cornelius Bliss.

Temple wasn't his real name, though he had been using it for the last ten years. Most people in his hometown of Meridian, Mississippi, would remember him as Levi Stuckey, the boy who'd mysteriously disappeared following the hanging of his father from the iron rails of Stuckey's Bridge. His father was Thomas Stuckey. He wasn't Levi's real father, but when someone back in those days assumed he was, Levi never bothered to correct them. As a matter of fact, Stuckey wasn't that man's real name, either. He took it from one of his victims, a man named Carter Stuckey. Carter Stuckey had spent the night at Thomas's inn on his way to deliver a trunk to Vicksburg—a trunk full of gold. Not many visitors ever left that inn, especially visitors who carried great wealth. Carter Stuckey fit that description, meeting his demise for being a deliveryman. Thomas Stuckey never got to enjoy the gold he stole, though. He was strung up for murder before he even viewed the sparkling contents of the trunk.

Following Thomas's hanging, twelve-year-old Levi disappeared with the trunk. He took a horse and wagon and rode away from Meridian with the trunk, and he didn't leave a trace.

After he fled, he dropped the name Stuckey so he'd never be associated with Thomas, Carter, or the missing trunk of gold. He considered taking back his given name, but he didn't want to be linked to the sack of crap who owned that name, either. It had been so long since he'd used his real name, he could barely remember what it was. So, after a quick deliberation, he took the name of the only man he'd ever trusted, the sheriff of Lauderdale County—J.R. Temple. Yes, Temple was a good name, a good name from a good man. Levi always felt a tinge of remorse for disappearing and leaving Sheriff Temple to wonder what happened to him, but at the time he didn't have a choice. He deserved more in life than a stolen name and a tainted past with murderers, drunks, and whores. The gold could give him the future he wanted.

Since the moment he left Lauderdale County, Levi had spent every waking hour infiltrating the inner circle of high society, and as of tonight, he had finally arrived. So far, this seemed a very good place to be. He sipped imported sparkling champagne as he socialized with gentlemen in expensive tuxedos, beautiful women adorned with exceptional jewels, and even a few servants who scurried around catering to the social elite. Though he wasn't born into this circle, and he thought most of them idiots who were beneath him, he felt at home here. He was finally receiving the respect he deserved.

As the orchestra struck up a lively ragtime tune, Levi walked toward the patio door to step outside and get a breath of fresh air. His heels clicked on the marble floor as he passed velvet chaise lounges and crystal chandeliers. The leaded-art glass was a sight to behold and the classical details of the mansion were breathtaking. He would have a house this fine someday.

He found the patio alit with lanterns and

twinkling holiday lights, flanked by sweeping staircases that led down to the beach. The half moon shone brightly in the winter sky, and an ocean breeze rustled through his dark blond hair. He closed his eyes for a moment and enjoyed the gentle wind on his face. He took a deep breath of the ocean draft. It smelled like fresh linen hung on the line. He opened his eyes and looked around. Baskets filled with late-blooming roses were spaced intermittently around the cement patio. Other than the fragrant flowers, he found the patio nearly empty. Everyone was inside on the dance floor celebrating the arrival of the new year. Everyone except that brunette he had been eyeing all evening.

He had noticed her hours earlier, the moment she entered the front door. She was petite but floated into the room like she owned the place, all willowy with a smoky air about her. Her charcoal-lined eyes were dark and seductive, hiding playfully behind the rim of her extravagant black velvet hat. When she walked, the long, white ostrich feather on top of her hat danced with each step. He found her movements intoxicating.

She wore the most luxurious mink stole he had ever seen, and when she removed it, she looked like a Grecian goddess. Her empire-waist dress flowed to the floor, the black velvet bodice cut low enough to make every man in the room stop and stare. The black fan she fluttered in front of her face made her even more exotic. Levi had attempted to approach her a few times throughout the evening, but she was always surrounded by admirers and he couldn't get close enough to utter a single word. Out here on the patio, she was again with a gentleman.

Levi stepped to the edge of the patio and placed his fingers on the railing. She had her back against the railing, being courted by some wealthy boy in a man's suit. Levi snickered. *These rich boys don't know how to seduce a woman*, he thought. *They think they can have anything they want, including a woman, simply because their fathers gave them money.*

He remained still and looked out to the sea. The moon illuminated a path of white on the dark water. The reflection went all the way to the horizon. He absentmindedly reached into his jacket pocket and pulled out his silver lighter. He flipped it open and closed over and over with one hand. He kept stealing glances to his left at the couple, wondering if he should interrupt them. The rich boy stumbled forward a little, almost falling onto the woman. He seemed to be more than a little drunk. Levi held his breath and waited for the woman to say something, hoping he'd be able to tell whether or not she needed him to intervene.

When she spoke, her voice had a deep rasp with the slightest Southern drawl. Why did that not surprise him? He felt a stirring in his loins and glanced again at the couple.

"Mr. Goodyear, I'm flattered by your attention, but don't you think we should be going back inside now? Your friends are surely looking for you."

The boy caught his balance, stood up straight, and countered, "No, they're not looking for me. They're having their own fun…just like we should." The boy leaned in for a kiss, but the woman turned her face to the left and looked directly into Levi's eyes. She smiled faintly.

It was not the plea of a woman needing assistance that he'd been expecting to see. The expression he saw on her face was one of confidence and power. This woman didn't need his help. She was more than capable of fending off a drunken suitor. Levi watched her as she scowled and playfully pushed on the boy's chest to back him away.

"Really, Mr. Goodyear, that's enough for now." She pushed harder on his chest.

The boy shrugged and mumbled something Levi couldn't make out. The woman pulled her fur around her shoulders and narrowed her eyes at Levi, suggesting he should mind his own business. She turned the boy toward the open doorway, tucked her arm into the crook of his elbow, and led him toward the ballroom. As the two made their way to the door, a woman's bloodcurdling scream came from the direction of the beach.

Levi and the couple turned toward the ocean, attempting to see the source of the screaming through the palm trees that lined the patio, but it was impossible. The screaming continued. People began streaming out of the ballroom, asking what was going on, and men sprinted down the stairs on both sides of the patio, hurrying toward the sound.

Levi turned and looked at the alluring woman, whose young suitor had left her standing alone while he joined the other men heading to the beach.

She stared into Levi's eyes with no expression.